"I'm your secretary—not your slave!"

"Don't push me too far, Kate," Luke warned, "or you won't be my secretary much longer!"

"Fine!" Kate snatched up her bag and marched over to the coat stand.

"Where do you think you're going?"

"Where do *you* think!" Kate said, dragging on her coat. "I'm going to find an employer who'll appreciate me—one who doesn't communicate in grunts. I'm afraid I don't respond to grunts."

"Do I have to go down on bended knee every time I want something?"

"A simple 'please' would do."

"I suppose this means I'll have to get my own coffee," Luke said with a martyred sigh.

Jessica Hart was born in Ghana, but grew up in an Oxfordshire village. Her father was a civil engineer working overseas, so by the time she left school, she'd been to East Africa, South Africa, Papua New Guinea and Oman—and had acquired incurably itchy feet. She's had a haphazard series of jobs, including production assistant at a theater, research assistant, waitress, teaching English, cook on an outback property—in England, Egypt, Kenya, Jakarta and Australia, respectively. She's also worked with Operation Raleigh, selecting Venturers for expeditions, which took her to Cameroon and Algeria. Jessica now lives in England, where her hobbies are limited to eating, drinking and traveling, preferably to places where she'll find good food or desert or tropical rain.

Books by Jessica Hart

HARLEQUIN ROMANCE
3213—THE TROUBLE WITH LOVE
3231—WOMAN AT WILLAGONG CREEK

Don't miss any of our special offers. Write to us at the following address for information on our newest releases.

Harlequin Reader Service
P.O. Box 1397, Buffalo, NY 14240
Canadian address: P.O. Box 603,
Fort Erie, Ont. L2A 5X3

NO MISTAKING LOVE
Jessica Hart

Harlequin Books

TORONTO • NEW YORK • LONDON
AMSTERDAM • PARIS • SYDNEY • HAMBURG
STOCKHOLM • ATHENS • TOKYO • MILAN
MADRID • WARSAW • BUDAPEST • AUCKLAND

For David and Sally

Original hardcover edition published in 1992
by Mills & Boon Limited

ISBN 0-373-17140-4

Harlequin Romance first edition June 1993

NO MISTAKING LOVE

CHAPTER ONE

KATE would have known him anywhere.

The same dark, ruthless looks, the same unreadable eyes, the same hard expression illuminated by a swift, disconcerting smile. She hadn't seen him for ten years but there was no mistaking him. Luke Hardman. The first man who had ever kissed her.

He was standing on the far side of the room, watching the crowds pushing their way to the theatre bar. It was something in the way he stood that had first caught Kate's eye, a sort of callous assurance in the way he held himself that set him apart from the rest. The dark severity of his dinner-jacket suited his steely looks, Kate decided, remembering a time when he would have scorned to wear anything other than a leather jacket. He would never have been near a theatre in those days either; perhaps he had changed more than she thought.

His face was too harsh to be really handsome, but there was a dangerous attraction about him. Kate wasn't the only woman who had noticed him. She watched a girl catch his eye and send him a provocative smile, but he merely looked through her, not bothering to hide his bored indifference. No, Kate thought, Luke Hardman hadn't changed that much.

She turned slightly so that she could watch his reflection in the mirrors lining the bar. She didn't want him to catch her staring—although it was hardly likely that he would notice her now, any more than he had ten years ago.

'Sorry, this is the best I could do.' Serena appeared suddenly at Kate's elbow and handed her a warm gin and tonic. A sliver of lemon floated listlessly in the glass. 'We should have ordered them before the interval.'

When Kate only murmured thanks absently Serena followed the direction of her gaze. 'He's rather gorgeous, isn't he?'

'Who?'

'The man you're staring at in the mirror!' She glanced over her shoulder at Luke. 'He's even better in the flesh.'

'I haven't been staring,' Kate said, but was unable to prevent a betraying flush. She fished the lemon out of the glass and sucked it thoughtfully as her eyes went back to Luke. 'Actually, I think I recognise him.'

'Oh?' Serena looked at him with renewed interest. 'Who is he?'

'Just someone from the village,' Kate said as casually as she could. 'I haven't seen him since I was sixteen.'

'How come you never introduced me when I came to stay?' Serena demanded, pretending to be aggrieved. 'I've always liked that "mad, bad and dangerous to know" type!'

Kate laughed. 'I wouldn't have dared introduce anyone to Luke Hardman! He was much older than me; I hardly knew him. But I always noticed him. He was different from the other boys in the village.' She paused. 'He used to make me nervous.'

'You? Nervous?' Serena looked at her friend in astonishment. 'I've known you since we first went to boarding-school, Kate, and I don't think I've ever seen you nervous. You wouldn't be Kate if you weren't calm, cool and collected at all times!'

'I wasn't with Luke. He had eyes that could look right through you. I could never decide whether he frightened or fascinated me—a bit of both, I think.' Kate gave an embarrassed laugh. 'I used to go all gauche and tongue-tied if he was around. All it took was a sight of him crossing the road, and my heart would start jumping around—classic adolescent stuff!' she finished, ignoring the way her heart had leapt when she had first seen Luke tonight.

Serena was grinning. 'Kate, how sweet! I never knew you had a crush on anyone.'

'It wasn't a crush, exactly,' Kate said in an attempt to salvage her pride. 'I didn't even like him.

He was rude and unpleasant and he never cared what anyone thought of him.'

'He sounds irresistible!' said Serena. 'Why don't you go over and say hello?'

'No!' said Kate, too quickly. 'I mean, he wouldn't remember me.'

'I don't see why not.'

'I'm not exactly the memorable type, am I?' Kate contemplated her reflection with resignation. She had grown out of a plain and gawky adolescence into a quietly attractive girl, but she had long accepted that she was never going to be wildly beautiful. Only her unusual eyes, a deep tawny gold, gave any indication that there was more to Kate than her habitual air of cool poise suggested.

'Well, I don't know,' Serena said loyally. 'You don't stand out in a crowd, but you've got the sort of face that lingers in the memory, even though you can't quite work out why. Anyway, if you remember him so well there's a good chance he remembers you too.'

Kate shook her head, amused despite herself. 'I've got a better reason to remember him. What girl ever forgets her first kiss?'

'Kate!' Serena shrieked, so that everyone turned and stared at them. Even Luke glanced in their direction. Kate turned hastily so that her face was hidden from his view.

'Sshh!'

'Sorry,' Serena whispered, going to the other extreme. 'Honestly, Kate, you are a dark horse! Did he really kiss you? How romantic!'

'It wasn't romantic at all,' Kate said with some astringency.

'Well, tell me what happened, then,' Serena said eagerly.

Kate sighed. She should never have mentioned that wretched kiss. Serena would insist on hearing the whole story now!

'Do you remember that hot summer after we did our O levels?' When Serena nodded she went on. 'I went home as usual, but Veronique was in France that year and I didn't have any company. All the other kids in the village used to avoid me because I lived in the manor and went to public school, and that meant that I was a snob. Worse, my mother was French and a bit flighty!' Kate gave a wry smile. It was easy not to mind now, but at the time it had hurt.

'Anyway, in the end I latched on to a girl called Anne who lived a couple of miles away. I didn't like her all that much, but she was better than nobody. She had a sister called Helen.'

Kate paused, remembering Helen and that long, hot summer.

'Well?' Serena prompted.

'Helen was having a fling with Luke Hardman,' Kate continued, almost reluctantly. 'Having a bit of rough, she used to call it,' she remembered with distaste. 'Her parents would have been furious if they'd found out, so Anne and I used to be roped in as alibis. Helen would pretend to come riding with us. We'd go down to the woods so she could meet Luke, and then Anne and I would be sent off for a couple of hours.'

Kate could still remember the *frisson* she had felt when Luke had smiled up at Helen, the look on his face as he'd pulled her off her horse. There had been an earthy sexuality about them that had made Kate uncomfortably aware of her own innocence. Luke had never even noticed she was there.

'Helen was all over him,' she continued. 'But she'd come back and sneer at him behind his back because he didn't hold his knife properly or something equally stupid. I hated that.'

'She sounds a bitch,' Serena said frankly. 'Did Luke know what she was like?'

Kate shrugged. 'You could never tell what Luke thought, but he found out soon enough. We were due to go riding one day and meet Luke down in the woods as usual, when Helen strolled in and said she wasn't coming, she'd been invited to the south of France and the men were more sophisticated down there. I asked her if she was going to tell Luke and she just laughed and said we should let him wait, he'd get the message soon enough. I'll never forget the way she laughed.'

'What did you do?'

'Anne was all for doing as Helen said, but I couldn't let him sit there and wait. It sounds stupid, but I hated the thought of him being humiliated. It would be like watching a tiger doing tricks. So I went down to the woods by myself and told him Helen wasn't coming.'

'Was he upset?'

'He was angry. Not shouting and raving, but just cold anger in his eyes. It was terrifying. I wished I hadn't gone then, because he seemed to notice me for the first time. He asked if I'd been sent to report back on how devastated he was, and when I said no he said had I come to offer myself as a consolation prize.' Kate's cheeks burned with the memory. 'It was awful. I tried to back off but he caught me with one hand and pulled me back.'

She glanced involuntarily down at her wrist, as if it still bore the imprint of his fingers. His hands had been very strong, his grip like steel as he had forced her chin up.

'Is that when he kissed you?' Serena asked, agog. They were both oblivious to the hubbub going on around them.

Kate nodded.

Serena glanced over at Luke and then leant closer to Kate. 'What was it like?' she whispered. 'Do you remember?'

Do you remember? Kate's eyes deepened to amber. She would never forget. Her feeling of terrified exhilaration as he had jerked her back into his arms was still vivid. The roughness of his hands against her skin, the unexpected warmth of his lips, the bitter anger in his eyes: Kate remembered them all. She remembered the dappled shade of the woods on that still, hot afternoon and the damp smell of earth beneath her feet.

She had never been kissed before. She hadn't known how strong a man's body could be, or how lips could be firm and fierce and persuasive all at the same time. She hadn't known about the trembling, treacherous excitement as he slid his hands slowly, lingeringly, down her bare arms, had never guessed at the ache of need that could swamp fear and dislike at the mere touch of his mouth.

Oh, yes, she remembered all right. Out of the corner of her eye Kate could see Luke. He looked bored and irritable, but his mouth was just as she remembered.

'It was just a kiss,' she said. She had never been kissed like that again.

'Oh.' It was clear that Serena was disappointed. 'Did he say anything to you afterwards?'

She had stared up at him as he had released her, shaken and dazed by the strength of her own reaction. Luke's eyes had been narrowed as if he was taken aback at suddenly finding her in his arms, and he had stepped back abruptly. Kate had read disgust in the gesture, and she had flinched as the stinging slap of humiliation had hit her with the force of a blow.

'He said, "Go home, Catherine, and grow up,"' Kate said slowly, reliving that devastating moment before she had turned and stumbled away from the contempt in his eyes.

'Catherine? Is that what he called you?' Serena asked, diverted. 'I thought you were always Kate.'

'Not at home. My mother always called me Catherine in the French way, and I was known as Catherine in Chittingdene. It was only when I went away to school that I became Kate to you lot.'

'I see.' Serena risked another glance at Luke. 'What happened next time you met him?'

'I never saw him again. He left the village a few days later. I don't know if he ever went back. Dad died a couple of months later and my mother couldn't wait to sell the manor and take us to France, so I never went back to Chittingdene. This is the first time I've seen him since.'

'I wonder if he would recognise you,' Serena said thoughtfully.

'Not a chance. Remember what I was like at sixteen, Serena? All bottle-bottom glasses and straggly hair! I've changed a lot since then, thank goodness. There's no way he'd recognise me. It's not as if I'm like Helen.'

'Why, what was she like?'

'She was——' Kate broke off, staring into the mirror, where Luke's face had lightened as a woman walked towards him. She laid her hand on his arm possessively, and took the drink that he handed her, apparently unconcerned that she had kept him waiting.

'See for yourself,' Kate said in an odd, toneless voice. 'That's Helen with him now.'

At eighteen, Helen had had a golden, provocative beauty, and the past ten years had merely added gloss and a subtle exoticism to her looks. She had slanting green eyes and silver-blonde hair that fell in a glittering, rippling fall to her waist. In a short strapless turquoise dress, she looked literally breathtaking.

'But that's Helen Slayne, isn't it?'

'That's right.' Kate looked at Serena in surprise. 'Why, do you know her?'

'Hardly! But she's a famous model. I've seen her in all sorts of things. That hair's a sort of trademark. I suppose you wouldn't have seen her while you've been in France. She's stunning, isn't she?'

'Yes,' said Kate flatly. 'She always was.'

There was a dull ache in her chest. Why was she so surprised to see Helen here with him? It was stupid to feel disappointed because Luke had evidently allowed himself to be taken in by that glittering beauty a second time. Why expect him to have had more pride? It was none of her business if he'd chosen to make a fool of himself again.

With Helen standing next to him, Luke wasn't going to be noticing anyone else in the room. Kate turned round and allowed herself to study him properly. It was strange that after all this time everything about him should be so familiar. The way he stood, the way he turned his head, the hard line of his mouth...especially his mouth... There had always been an air of arrogance about him, a kind of reckless pride. How *could* he stand there, smiling at Helen like that after the way she had treated him?

As if she had shouted it aloud, Luke lifted his head and stared over Helen's shoulder straight into the unguarded criticism in Kate's eyes.

Kate's heart lurched alarmingly as she found herself staring into those slate-grey eyes. He was nowhere near her, but she felt skewered by that cold, hard look. She wanted to look away, but the eyes held her immobile. They might have been alone in the room. The crush and hubbub in the bar faded to insignificance, Serena and Helen were forgotten. There was only a narrowed slate-grey gaze and the nervous jolt of her heart.

And then a couple in front of her stepped back to let someone through *en route* to the bar and cut Luke from view.

Kate swallowed and dropped her eyes, annoyed to find herself flushing.

'Do you think he did recognise you after all?' Serena said excitedly. She had watched the look Luke and Kate had exchanged with interest.

'No.' Kate sounded curt, but she was having difficulty bringing her heart under control again. It kept jumping around in an alarmingly erratic manner. 'No, I don't think so,' she said again, more lightly. The eyes had been as unreadable as ever, but she would swear that there had been no recognition in them, only a speculative sort of contempt.

To Kate's intense relief, a bell began to ring insistently over the noise of the crowd just as Serena opened her mouth to pursue the matter.

'Come on, drink up,' she said, taking a hasty swig of her gin. 'The second half's about to start.'

They joined the queue shuffling noisily back into the auditorium. Serena seemed to have forgotten Luke, and was telling Kate about her not-so-subtle attempts to get her handsome neighbour to notice her. Wedged in the middle of the crowd, Kate rolled her eyes and laughed at her friend. She had a warm, arresting smile that lit up her quiet face—but which switched off abruptly as she found herself looking once more into Luke Hardman's hard eyes.

He and Helen were unhurriedly finishing their drinks while the crowd pushed past them. Luke Hardman had never been a man to waste time standing in a queue with everyone else.

Someone was pushing Kate from behind, but she hardly noticed. Luke had lifted his glass in a silent toast and sent her a swift, mocking smile that flamed the colour in her cheeks.

'Can you get a move on? You're blocking the door and the play's starting in a couple of minutes!' The impatient voice behind her jerked Kate out of her trance and she looked quickly away from Luke.

'Oh—er—sorry,' she muttered as she hurried to catch up with Serena.

She had been enjoying the play, but she sat through the second half without hearing a word. Seeing Luke again after all these years had left her feeling edgy and unsettled. She tried to concentrate on the stage, but her mind was tugged back irresistibly to that hot afternoon and the woods and how it had felt when Luke had pulled her round into his arms.

Suddenly Kate became aware of a storm of applause around her, and, as Serena gave her an odd look, hastily began to clap. There was no point in dwelling on the past, she told herself, still thinking about Luke. It had been a remarkable coincidence, seeing him here tonight, but it was unlikely that she would ever see him again.

Even so, she couldn't help searching the crowds for a glimpse of him as they left the theatre, slowing her steps deliberately until Serena asked her what the matter was.

'Nothing,' said Kate, quashing a feeling of inexplicable disappointment. He must have gone already.

'You're awfully quiet,' Serena said suspiciously.

'My contact lenses are killing me,' Kate lied as they headed towards the Underground. 'It was so smoky in that bar.'

They flipped their season tickets open at the gate and joined the crowd filing down the escalators. 'How's the job hunting going?' Serena asked, turning round from the step below to look up at Kate. 'Have you managed to find what you want yet?'

Kate forced her mind back to the present and her most pressing need to find a job. 'Not yet, but I've got an interview for tomorrow that sounds promising.' She rummaged in her handbag as they stepped off the escalator. 'I've got the ad here. What do you think?'

Serena took the newspaper cutting. '"*Parlez-vous français?*"' she read the heading. 'Well, you can certainly do that, Kate!

A bilingual PA is required for dynamic director of this successful company. Fluent French required, plus excellent secretarial skills, preferably with director-level experience. Must be confident, super-efficient and free to travel.

'Kate, it sounds perfect!' Her eye fell on the salary quoted at the bottom of the advertisement and she whistled. 'I wouldn't mind pay like that!'

'I know.' Kate took the cutting back and they walked slowly down the platform. 'It sounds a bit too good to be true, doesn't it? But I need to get something soon. If I'd realised how difficult it would be to get a good job here I don't think I'd have given up my job in Dijon quite so quickly!'

'You're not regretting coming back to England, are you?'

'No.' Kate shook her head. 'I'd been in that job four years. It was time to move on. Solange coming to school in England gave me the impetus to make the break.'

'I do think it's a bit of cheek for Veronique and Alain to go swanning off to the Ivory Coast and expect you to look after their daughter for them,' Serena said, indignant on Kate's behalf.

'They'd have had to send Solange to boarding-school anyway,' Kate said mildly. 'Veronique always had this thing about making sure Solange

is bilingual by sending her to school in England
for a year, just as she had to do. It just seems a
convenient time when Alain's job takes him to
Africa for a year.'

'Convenient for them that you're prepared to
give up your job to be near her,' Serena commented tartly.

'Oh, Solange is just an excuse, really. I could
hardly tell my mother that I can't stand her new
husband, could I? It was all getting rather uncomfortable with Thierry and me being extra
polite to each other, and poor Maman stuck in
between. She'd be terribly upset if she thought
I'd left home because of Thierry, so I said I was
coming to keep Solange company. It's partly true,
anyway. I feel rather sorry for Solange: I remember what it's like being at boarding-school
with no one around to take you out at weekends
and make a fuss of you. I remember what it's
like being a foreigner too. I always felt French in
England, and English in France, so I sym-
pathise. After all, I am her aunt—and it's hardly
a great sacrifice to come back to England.'

Kate stuck her hands in the pockets of her
jacket and smiled at Serena. 'My mother thinks
I'm being wonderful, Veronique and Alain think
I'm being wonderful, but really I'm just being
selfish. I never really settled in Dijon; I only
stayed because I didn't think Maman would be
able to cope by herself—you know how imprac-

tical she is!—and once I had a good job it seemed so silly to give it up. But Maman's got Thierry to look after her now, and if the truth was known she'd probably much rather I wasn't around looking quite so grown up!' Kate gazed reflectively at the huge poster on the other side of the tracks urging her to throw caution to the winds and jump on the next plane to the Caribbean. 'It's all worked out very well. I've missed England these last few years. I should have come back before.'

'Well, I hope you stay.' Serena squeezed her arm affectionately. 'It's good to have you back. All you need now is that job!'

CHAPTER TWO

THE lift was lined with mirrors. Kate checked her reflection, tugging her jacket down and smoothing an invisible strand of hair from her cheek.

She was reluctant to admit to herself how much she needed this job. Living in London was proving a lot more expensive than she had envisaged, and the rent was due on her flat soon. Besides, she was tired of trailing round agencies. Friends like Serena teased her, but she was an orderly person and missed the routine of work.

The girl in the mirror looked back at her critically. She was trim and neat in a grey suit and high-necked white blouse, and her thick brown hair was twisted up and held away from her face by a tortoiseshell clasp.

She looked crisp and efficient—and dull, Kate decided as clear eyes gazed back at her a little wistfully. No wonder Luke Hardman hadn't remembered her! It wasn't as if there was anything wrong with her, but there was nothing very special either. She was just Kate: cool, capable Kate.

An ideal secretary, in fact, she reminded herself sensibly as the doors slid open on to a thickly carpeted corridor. Stepping out, Kate was met by a harassed-looking girl with wavy red hair.

'Miss Finch? I'm Paula Stephens. We spoke on the phone.' She seemed relieved by Kate's businesslike air. 'I had hoped to explain a bit about this job before you met the managing director, but he's in a tearing hurry today, so would you mind if I introduced you to him first and then we had a word later?'

'Of course not,' Kate said politely, wondering if it was the managing director who had reduced her to such a jittery state.

Paula led her along the corridor and into an office. It was a large, bright room, equipped with all the latest technology. 'This would be your room,' she said, and then lowered her voice. 'That's *his* office in there,' she said in a conspiratorial whisper, nodding her head at a door on the far side of the room.

With a visible attempt to steel herself Paula went over and knocked. 'Miss Finch is here to see you,' she said nervously.

Kate heard an impatient voice say, 'All right, all right. Tell her to come in,' before Paula stood back and, with a look that was suspiciously sympathetic, gestured her inside and shut the door behind her.

She found herself in a vast, high-ceilinged room with a window that looked out over the elegant Knightsbridge street below. For a moment she hesitated, confused by the fact that she seemed to be alone in the room, and then the voice spoke again, deep and abrupt.

'Sit down, if you're staying. I've just got to finish this.'

It came from a high-backed revolving chair, which had been turned away from the desk to face the window. Kate raised one eyebrow at the man's rudeness and chose an upright chair set against the wall. Lifting it forward, she set it in front of the desk and sat down composedly, smoothing her skirt over her knees and folding her hands calmly in her lap. The squashy leather chairs looked inviting, but she would be at a distinct disadvantage if she sank into one of them, and she had a strong feeling that she was going to need all the advantages she could get in dealing with this man.

Minutes passed. The only indication of another presence in the room was the sound of turning pages from behind the chair. Kate waited, but her lips tightened disapprovingly. She was tempted to get up and leave, but a stern, sensible voice inside her reminded her about the fat salary, and the rent due, and the imprudence of chucking in her chances of a good job by storming out, and no doubt causing an embarrassing scene.

Eventually he spoke. 'I gather from my personnel manager that you claim to speak French?'

'I *do* speak French,' Kate corrected him with frosty emphasis.

'I've seen a succession of girls who say they speak French, but in fact can barely muster an O level between them. They're all *just a little rusty.*' He mimicked the feminine tones contemptuously. 'Frankly, I don't want to waste any more time on you unless you can speak French fluently.'

'I wasn't aware that you'd wasted any time on me,' Kate said with a slight edge to her voice. 'However, I can assure that I *can* speak French. I'm bilingual.'

'Prove it.'

'I beg your pardon?'

'I said, prove it. Say something in French!'

'Well . . . what would you like me to say?' Kate asked carefully.

'What does it matter?' he retorted, impatient and irritable. 'Anything. *N'importe quoi.*'

His French was pronounced with such an appalling accent that Kate's tawny eyes gleamed suddenly gold.

'*N'importe quoi*?' she repeated. He obviously didn't speak French himself, so she could allow herself free rein! 'It's a little hard to know what to say to a chair,' she continued in fluent French and with a deceptively calm intonation. 'I've never had to address one before. In France we have the courtesy to get up and greet people when they come into the room, but obviously things are a little different here! Frankly, if it weren't for the fact that I'd really rather like this job I would have got up and left ten minutes ago! Not that I'm sure now that I *would* like it if it means working for someone who can't even be bothered to turn round when I talk to him,' she went on reflectively. 'I can't see that there's any excuse for those kind of sheer bad manners——'

She broke off abruptly as the chair swung round.

'That's fine, thank you,' he said in such a non-committal tone that Kate was convinced, not without some relief, that he hadn't understood a word.

She still couldn't see his face. His dark head was bent over a report and he was making neat notes in the margin with a pencil. Kate's eyes narrowed at the sheer arrogance of the gesture. However this man had got to be managing director, it certainly hadn't been through charm!

Then he laid his pencil very neatly beside the report and looked up.

It was Luke Hardman.

Kate's heart stopped. For that long, shocked moment as she stared incredulously into the flat blue-grey eyes all she could think about was whether it would ever start beating again.

It seemed an age, but was probably no more than a few seconds before the sharpening of

Luke's unnerving gaze jerked her heart back into action.

'Is something the matter?' he demanded, brusque suspicion in his voice as he took in her expression of stunned disbelief.

Kate struggled to regain her composure. There was absolutely no recognition in his eyes; she could see that now. It was just that he had occupied her thoughts so much since she had seen him at the theatre that it seemed incredible that he had not been just as aware of her, and as astonished to find the gauche, clumsy girl who had stumbled away from his kiss sitting in front of him now. As astonished as she was to find that the village rebel had somehow transformed himself into a successful businessman! It was the last thing she would have expected.

But the awareness was one-sided now, just as it had been last night, just as it had been ten years ago. Kate should have been glad, but a quite irrational feeling of pique at finding herself so utterly unmemorable helped her to pull herself together.

'I'm sorry if I was staring. I was merely surprised to find myself addressing a man instead of a chair,' she said, pleased at the cool way she was able to meet his eyes. Preoccupied with the shock of coming face to face with him again so unexpectedly, Kate had forgotten that she was here for an interview, but Luke evidently had not.

'Doesn't take much to surprise you, does it?' Luke said with something of a sneer. He reached out and pulled a sheet of paper off the pile in front of him; Kate recognised it as the CV she had sent to Paula Stephens and wondered if anything about her name would jog his memory.

He was frowning as he scrutinised her details. Kate sat, outwardly calm, dreading the moment when he would look up and recognise her, but he only grunted non-committally as he tossed her CV back dismissively on to the pile.

Sitting back in his chair, he twirled a pen between his fingers and studied her with opaque slate eyes narrowed appraisingly. Kate forced herself to return his look with composure, and her chin tilted in instinctive response to the challenge in his silence.

'Well, you can speak French, I'll give you that...what's your name?' Luke leant forward and turned over the CV. 'Kate...yes, I'll give you that, Kate,' he said at last. His voice was as hard as his expression. 'But speaking French doesn't make you a good secretary. What about typing and shorthand? Can you do all that?'

'It says there that I can,' Kate said, nodding at the CV. She had recovered from those first few moments of shocked disbelief and was fast losing her temper. He obviously had no idea how to treat people! The cynical indifference that had so intimidated her ten years ago still had the power to affect her, but now her reaction was one of annoyance instead of mortification. She wasn't a shy sixteen-year-old any longer, and Luke would find out, surprise or no surprise, that she wasn't prepared to put up with it.

'I know it *says* you can,' Luke was saying. 'It says you've got all sorts of impressive-looking skills to boast about.' He tapped the CV with a sneer. 'Bilingual shorthand, bilingual typing, exceptional speeds... It all looks very good on paper, but I want to know if you can actually do any of it!'

'I wouldn't have put them down if I couldn't,' Kate said, keeping a tight rein on her temper with some difficulty.

'Oh, really? In my experience, women have a fine disregard for the truth when it suits them! I'm sure you can type, I'm just not convinced that you haven't increased your speeds—oh, just an extra ten or twenty words a minute!—to make your CV look more impressive.'

'I have done nothing of the sort!' Kate said icily. Looking up from her CV, Luke was in time to catch the flash of fury in her eyes, brightening their brown depths to a fierce gold and making the quiet face suddenly vivid. He frowned, the strong brows drawing together as if a chord had been struck, but Kate was too angry to notice.

'You can't have a working relationship with someone you distrust on principle!' she swept on.

'If you're that concerned about speeds it's simple enough to arrange for tests, but, frankly, if you're not prepared to take my word I might as well leave now!'

'All right, all right, calm down,' Luke said irritably, throwing his pen on to the desk. 'I'll assume you're as pure as the driven snow and that all your qualifications are quite as phenomenal as they appear, if that'll make you any happier.' His unnerving eyes inspected her thoughtfully. 'But if you're such a perfect secretary, why do you want this job so badly?'

'I'm not sure that I do!' Kate said, still angry.

'Oh? I was under the impression that you wanted this job—at least enough to make sure you didn't get up and walk out the way you wanted to when faced with my appalling manners.'

Kate looked wary. She had said something like that . . . but surely he hadn't understood?

'I think you should know,' Luke answered her unspoken question with a sardonic look, 'that, although my accent is poor, I understand French perfectly well.'

'Oh,' she said uncomfortably.

'Oh, indeed,' he mocked, and Kate knew that he was enjoying her discomfiture. To her annoyance, she coloured faintly.

'Well?' he prompted.

'I'm sorry if I was rude,' she said stiffly.

'I don't mind your being rude, but I can't be bothered with a secretary who's going to sulk if *I'm* rude, or lecture me on my manners. I've got too much to do to worry about trivia like that!'

'It's not trivia,' Kate said before she could help herself. 'If you want people to work for you you've got to treat them like human beings.'

'I said I didn't want to be lectured on my manners!' Luke snapped, but Kate was unrepentant.

'Ill-mannered people never do!'

His dark brows drew together in a dangerous scowl. 'Do you want this job or not?'

Did she? Kate felt as if she had been suddenly brought up short. Could she really contemplate working for Luke Hardman? It would be hideously embarrassing if he ever recognised her, but how likely was that? If he hadn't remembered her by now he probably never would. When Paula Stephens had described the job on the phone it had sounded so much more interesting than the other jobs she had contemplated.

Kate stared down at her hands. It would be wonderful to have a good salary again, too. Luke was rude and unpleasant, but she was surprised at how little he frightened her now. He would be infuriating, of that she had no doubt, but she was oddly certain that she could handle him.

With a little shock she realised that she found the prospect exciting. Steady, sensible Kate had always been content with security and routine, had never yearned for excitement, but suddenly it seemed natural to be sitting here contemplating working closely with Luke with a small thrill of disbelief. Only last night she had seen him for the first time in ten years, and now she was calmly considering spending most of her days with him!

'Well?' he demanded again impatiently. 'Make up your mind!'

Kate looked up from her hands. 'Yes,' she said. 'I do want it.'

'You don't seem very sure.'

'I am sure.'

'Why?' he asked abruptly. 'According to your CV, you had a good job with a wine exporter in Dijon. What made you give that up? You're not the kind of girl who chucks in a job on a whim, are you?'

'No,' Kate said in a level voice. 'My niece has been sent to boarding-school in England while her parents are in Africa. She doesn't know anyone else here, so I said I'd be around to take her out for weekends or in case there were any problems. That meant coming back to England and finding a job here.'

'Very worthy,' Luke jeered. 'Not many aunts would give up a good job to go and work in another country just to be near a niece. There must be some other reason for all this altruism.'

Kate flushed angrily at his tone. 'I'd been thinking about coming back to England anyway—for personal reasons,' she added, seeing his brows raised in enquiry. There was no need to go into details about her mother's new husband. It was none of his business.

'Hmmnn,' he grunted. 'I suppose that means boyfriend trouble?'

'No.' Kate refused to elaborate. 'This just seemed a good opportunity to come back,' she said with a note of finality.

Luke was tapping his pen on the desk. 'How long had you been living in France? I assume you're English, with a name like Kate Finch?'

'I'm half-French and half-English. I grew up in England; but after my father died my mother took me back to Dijon. We must have lived there about ten years now.'

'I see. And what happens if you get homesick for France and want to go back there?'

'I won't. I grew up in England; it feels like home to me. I still have schoolfriends here, so it's not as if I'm all alone. In any case, I wouldn't leave Solange, my niece, here on her own.'

Pushing back his chair, Luke stood up and prowled over to the window. 'My last secretary left before Christmas, and I'm sick of a succession of temps who all burst into tears as soon as I raise my voice. At least you don't look as if you'll do that.'

'Certainly not,' Kate said crisply.

'What did Paula tell you about the job?' he asked suddenly.

'She said it was very much a personal assistant's role. You wanted an efficient secretary, but also someone who was prepared to get involved so that you could delegate some of your responsibilities when you were away.'

'That's about it. I don't want someone who's going to sit and file her nails all day!'

Involuntarily Kate glanced down at her hands. They were slim and elegant, but she had always kept her nails cut short and neat for practical reasons.

'Do you know what we do here at LPM?'

'I know the letters stand for London Project Management,' Kate said cautiously. 'I gathered you were engineering consultants of some kind.'

Luke nodded, moving away from the window to pace about the room, hands thrust in his pockets, as if he had too much energy to sit still any longer.

'We dress it up in nice language for the clients, but we're more or less Mr Fixit on major building projects. There are an enormous number of interests involved in any one project—architects, consultants, contractors, subcontractors, suppliers, you name it—and we act as a liaison between them all, representing the client. That means we have to know exactly what's going on at any one point, sort out any problems, and make sure our client is getting what he's paid for.

'I used to spend a lot of my time on site, but the firm has expanded in the past couple of years, and I delegate most of the technical work now. My main concern nowadays is getting new contracts, especially now we're extending into the international market. That's why I need a proper PA. I've got to have someone capable of holding the fort while I'm away—although I might need you to come with me sometimes.' His pacing had brought him back to the desk. 'Are you free to travel?'

'Yes, except for when Solange comes to me for the weekend.'

'Nobody else likely to make a fuss if you're away a lot? No boyfriend lurking in the wings, ready to sulk if you don't leave work at five-thirty on the dot?'

'No,' said Kate.

It was strange, she thought, how he could be so familiar, and yet a stranger at the same time. The brusque, aggressive businessman was new to her, but the turn of his head or the set of his mouth would bring back vivid memories of the Luke she had known, a wilder, more reckless Luke. This man prowling around the room was harder and tougher, his rebelliousness channelled into impatient ambition and the old half-suspected vulnerability firmly vanquished by an

air of crisp efficiency and clear indifference to
other people's opinions.

Luke was standing by the window again,
staring down at the street as he thought.

'You seem sensible enough,' he admitted
grudgingly. 'And you're the first person I've seen
who can speak French properly. We've done quite
a bit of work in the States and Australia, but I
want to move into Europe now. There are plenty
of opportunities opening up, and I want to be
the first in there. We're bidding for a big French
project at the moment, but, although I can
understand French, I can't speak it, so I badly
need an assistant who can. I also need someone
who's prepared to work as hard as I do without
whining or crying or droning on about her rights.
Is that clear?'

'Perfectly,' Kate said, a dry edge to her voice.

'I'm a difficult man to work for,' he warned.

'I'd gathered that,' murmured Kate.

'But in return,' Luke went on, ignoring her in-
terruption, 'you'll get a generous salary. I expect
you to earn it. I don't want you bleating that you
didn't know what I was going to be like or how
much work you'd have to do!'

'Are you offering me the job?' Kate sat up a
little straighter and fought down a feeling of
panic. What had she done?

'On a month's trial,' he said quickly. 'I want
to see those famous skills of yours in action

before I commit myself to paying you that kind of money every month.'

'Very well.'

Luke raised a sardonic eyebrow. 'Is that all you've got to say? *Very well?* You might sound a little more enthusiastic about getting the job!'

'You don't sound very enthusiastic about employing me,' Kate retorted, nettled by his grudging offer.

Over the desk their eyes met and clashed. Kate's cheeks were pink, and her brown eyes bright with antagonism. Luke glared at her, clearly unused to being answered back, and then, quite suddenly, the wrathful expression disappeared.

He walked back round his desk towards Kate, still sitting straight and prim in her upright chair. He had always moved like that, she thought irrelevantly, with that deliberate tread. It overwhelmed her with memories, like a series of flashcards flicking rapidly in front of her eyes: Luke walking down the quiet village street, Luke reaching up to pull Helen off her horse, Luke running his hand down Helen's bare arm in a gesture which had shaken Kate even then with a *frisson* of sexual awareness.

He was standing in front of her, studying her face intently. Kate had no choice but to look back at him as coolly as she could. Close to, he seemed bigger than she remembered, as if his frame had thickened out to lean, muscled strength. Those lines around his eyes had not been there before, and nor had the grooves in his cheeks. Luke might be successful now, but the last few years had not been easy ones.

'Stand up,' he ordered abruptly.

Kate raised her brows in unconscious hauteur, and he ground out, '*Please*!'

She stood.

Kicking the chair out of the way, Luke walked round her, studying her figure so impersonally that Kate felt herself quiver with anger.

'You'll do,' he said at last. 'You've got good legs and a neat figure, but you need to smarten yourself up a bit.'

'I wasn't aware that I was taking part in a beauty contest!' Kate's eyes flashed dangerously again, and Luke stiffened.

He turned her to face him properly and took her chin in one strong hand, forcing it up so that she had to look mutinously into penetrating slate eyes.

'I *thought* I recognised you,' he said.

CHAPTER THREE

KATE couldn't move. She stared helplessly up at Luke, waiting for the jeering contempt she was sure he would feel at recognising her.

Very carefully he undid the clip holding up her hair so that the thick brown tresses uncoiled and tumbled about her face. She could feel his fingers brush against her cheek and lift her hair, and was conscious suddenly of the lean, powerful body so close to hers.

Her eyes dropped and she stared woodenly at his tie. It was dark blue silk with a discreet golden crest. Why didn't he say something? How much would he remember about the plain, awkward girl she had been? Would he remember kissing her? Would he remember the way she had responded so eagerly? It must have been so obvious that it was her first kiss.

'You were at the theatre last night.'

'At the theatre?' Kate repeated stupidly. She had been so busy thinking about the past that she had forgotten about the meeting that had triggered all the memories.

'Don't pretend you don't remember! You were the girl who was looking daggers at me in the

theatre bar. I thought you looked familiar when
you came in, but it was only when you gave me
that look that I remembered where I'd seen you.
Tell me, what did I do to earn such disapproval?'

Kate felt her breath leak out with relief. He
hadn't remembered! Immediately the thought
that he might have done seemed ridiculous. She
stepped back to give herself time to gather her
wits together, and felt the wooden desk against
her thighs.

The thick hair tumbling about her face left her
feeling curiously vulnerable. She pushed it behind
her ears.

'I must have done something to offend you,'
Luke persisted. 'I couldn't mistake that fierce
look. It's not at all like your usual demure expression, and you didn't look at anyone else like
that. You kept that very nice smile for your
friend.'

There was a steely note to his voice, and Kate
swallowed. 'You didn't do anything to offend
me.'

'Then why the glare?'

'I...' Kate searched her mind feverishly for
some kind of reason that would satisfy him. 'I
thought you were someone I knew,' she said at
last, keeping as close to the truth as she dared.

'Is that why you were staring at me in the
mirror?'

Trust him to notice that! Faint colour tinged Kate's cheekbones. 'I was trying to decide whether I knew you or not.'

'And what did this unfortunate man who looks like me do to earn such a look?'

'I really don't think that's any of your business,' Kate said quellingly.

To her relief, and somewhat to her surprise, he let that go. 'I suppose that's why you looked so surprised when you saw me today?'

Didn't he miss anything? 'It just seemed an extraordinary coincidence to see you again.'

Luke's flat blue-grey stare held her immobile. 'I'm not a great believer in coincidence,' he said.

'You're *working* for him?' Serena's voice rose to a shriek. 'The same Luke Hardman you were telling me about last night? I thought you didn't like him?'

'You don't have to like your boss, do you?'

'It usually helps!'

'Well, I think I'll get used to him.' Kate had rushed home to telephone Serena with the news of her job. 'It's too good a job to turn down, Serena.'

'Does he know who you are? Or, rather, does he know that you know who he is?'

'No. He recognised me from last night, but not before.'

'I'm surprised he didn't recognise your name,' Serena said.

'It's not that surprising. If he remembers me at all it would be as Catherine Haddington-Finch, but I'm just plain Kate Finch on my CV. I dropped the Haddington when we went to France—it was too much for the French to cope with! And Finch isn't an unusual name. There's no reason why he should make any connection.'

'You hope!'

Kate made a face at the receiver. 'I'm sure he won't. I thought you'd be pleased that I've got a job at last!'

'I am, Kate. I just hope you don't regret tangling with this Luke Hardman again.'

Serena's words echoed ominously the following Monday as Kate took the lift up to the fourth floor. She hoped fervently that she was doing the right thing. Lying alone in the dark at night, she would shift uneasily, unsettled by memories of Luke and a vague sense that getting involved with him again—even on a strictly business basis—was asking for trouble.

But in the bright light of morning her reservations seemed ridiculous. Luke would never remember her; it was stupid to let one stupid incident in the past prevent her from taking on an interesting and well-paid job. Besides, Solange had come out of school for the weekend. She was still a little homesick, and missing her parents, and had been so delighted to have a familiar figure as a refuge from school that Kate's resolve to stay in England was strengthened.

She dressed with care for her first morning at work in a severely cut suit in a Prince of Wales check. It made her look formidably efficient and bolstered her confidence. She had a feeling she was going to need it.

Luke barely glanced at her as she went into the office and wished him good morning. His head was bent over a report, and a pile of papers on his desk bore witness to the fact that he had been there for some time already. His jacket was slung over a chair and he had loosened his tie to work in shirt-sleeves, the white cotton rolled up to reveal the dark hairs on his powerful forearms.

'Morning,' he said in a brusque voice. 'Glad to see you're here on time. I've got a lot to get through this morning.' He turned a page of the report and picked up a pen to make a note. 'Are you ready to start?'

Kate had made a point of arriving half an hour earlier than necessary, but now she wished she hadn't. It was clear that she would have to take a stand right away if he was to avoid his taking her for granted!

'I'd like a coffee first while I sort myself out,' she said firmly. 'I haven't even had time to find myself a notebook yet!'

'Oh, very well, but hurry up about it!'

Kate suppressed a sigh. It was no use expecting charm from Luke and she couldn't say that he hadn't warned her. 'Would you like a coffee, as I'm making one?' she asked.

Luke grunted and Kate, after looking at his bent head for a moment, turned and quietly left the room.

She returned a few minutes later, equipped with a shorthand notebook, a pen and a cup of coffee. She put this on her side of the desk, sat down, opened the notebook on her knee and calmly waited for Luke to notice her.

He looked up at last. 'Don't I get a coffee?'

'You didn't say you wanted one.'

'Yes, I did!'

'No,' she corrected him in patient tones. 'You grunted. I'm afraid I don't respond to grunts.'

Luke sighed irritably. 'Don't say I have to go down on bended knee every time I want you to do something!'

'A simple please would do.'

His martyred air slightly spoiled by a glower, Luke pushed back his chair and strode over to the door. 'I suppose I'll have to get my own coffee, then!' he said, evidently expecting Kate to jump to her feet, but she merely looked blandly back at him.

His previous secretaries had clearly been letting him get away with playing the tyrant, and she had no intention of doing the same. It wouldn't

do Luke Hardman any harm to come across a
bit of opposition for a change!

Reappearing with his own cup, he banged it
down on his desk with bad grace. 'Perhaps we
could begin?' he said, adding sarcastically, 'if
that's not too much trouble, of course!'

'I'm ready,' Kate said, annoyingly placid.

Casting her a fulminating glance, Luke began
to prowl about the room, hands jammed in his
trouser pockets, while he dictated at high speed.
His ideas were complex, but clear and obviously
well thought out, and he paused only occasionally to take a sip of coffee.

Kate's pen flew over her notebook as she tried
grimly to keep up, but she seized the opportunity
to interrupt him as he picked up his cup once
more.

'Do you think you could slow down a bit?'

Luke frowned at losing his train of thought.
'I thought you said you could do shorthand?'

'I can, but not at the speed of light!'

With a sigh he resumed at a more normal
speed.

It was easier to keep up, but Kate found herself
increasingly distracted by the way he flexed his
shoulders, by the suggestion of strength beneath
his cotton shirt or the coiled tension in the way
he moved.

He was standing over at the window, frowning
down at the traffic as he dictated. Kate glanced

up, the outlines emerging automatically from her pen, and let her eyes rest on the back of his dark head. There was a steely quality to Luke, evident in the very set of his head and the controlled lines of his body. If he had a vulnerable side he would take care to keep it well hidden, she decided. Did the hard features ever relax, the cold eyes soften in a smile? How would he look at the woman he loved?

'Read me back that last bit, will you?'

Kate started. 'What?'

'Would it be too much trouble to ask you to read back the last part of that sentence to me?' Luke said sarcastically, misinterpreting her hesitation.

She had been taking down his words so automatically that she had hardly taken in what he was saying. Now the shorthand squiggles danced in front of her eyes as she tried to make sense of what she had written.

'Um... ''The contractors are concerned that if the manufacturers loved——'' ' She broke off, flustered. The outline was unmistakable. She must have written that 'loved' without thinking.

Luke turned and stared at her. 'If the manufacturers what? Can't you concentrate for more than five minutes at a time? If I go any slower I'll fall asleep!'

'It's really not at all easy to follow you when you're prowling around or muttering at the window,' Kate said, disguising her guilt with an air of reproof. 'It would help if you sat down and spoke clearly.'

'Who's doing the dictation round here?' Luke demanded sourly, but he sat down again on the other side of the desk. 'Is that better?'

Kate ignored the irony in his voice. 'Much, thank you,' she said, but it wasn't really. This way he was much closer, and his front view was even more distracting than the back. Kate concentrated fiercely on her notebook and tried not to notice the cool, inflexible line of his mouth or the fingers twirling a pen in his frustration at having to sit still.

He let her go twenty minutes later, having dictated three more letters and several trenchant memos to his staff. There would be a few panic-stricken phone calls when they landed on their desks, Kate reflected, gathering up the papers from the desk and escaping gratefully to her own office.

Naturally organised, Kate was unworried by the amount of work Luke seemed to expect her to get through that morning. She settled herself down with the minimum of fuss, familiarised herself with the word processor and began to work her way through the enormous pile of letters, breaking off frequently to deal with phone calls for Luke. He had shut himself in his office and informed her that he didn't want to be disturbed before midday.

Frowning over a particularly obscure outline, Kate didn't look up immediately as the door to the outer office opened. It was probably one of the junior secretaries with some more post, she thought, and was about to look up with a friendly smile when a waft of exotic perfume reached her. She lifted her head in puzzlement to see who was sauntering over towards Luke's door.

It was Helen. With something of a shock Kate realised that she had been so taken up with seeing Luke again that she had forgotten about Helen.

How could she have forgotten that eclipsing beauty? Helen wore the briefest of black leather skirts, and a leather blouson jacket, slipping at one shoulder over a wispy top. It was a carefully careless look, and the effect with the loose blonde hair was dramatic.

The checked suit, which only that morning had seemed so smart and suitable, suddenly felt tight and dowdy. Kate looked at Helen and recognised with a twist of bitterness a vibrant sexiness that she would never, ever possess, no matter what she wore. She would look absurd dressed in such an outfit. Worse, she would be cold and uncomfortable.

If she had given Helen any thought she might have realised that Helen would be bound to turn up at the office at some stage. It was stupid not to have considered it. She had seen more of Kate than Luke, and might possibly remember her sister's little friend. She could spoil everything if she recognised her.

Kate cleared her throat. The last thing she wanted was to attract Helen's attention, but she could hardly let her barge in on Luke unannounced after all the fuss he had made about no interruptions.

She needn't have worried about being recognised. Helen was not the kind of girl who wasted much time noticing other women, particularly not plain, boring ones who were patently no threat. She turned with insulting unconcern, and the green eyes flickered over Kate without interest.

Kate could see herself just as Helen saw her: a boringly efficient-looking type in a prissy suit, with dull brown hair tied back and minimal make-up. There could hardly have been more of a contrast between them.

'I'm afraid Mr Hardman has asked not to be disturbed,' she said, for a moment almost resenting her role as cool, competent secretary.

Helen laughed confidently and shook back her glorious hair. 'He won't mind being disturbed by me,' she said, laying her hand on the door and opening it. 'Will you, darling?' She half stepped inside, leaning back against the door in a deliberately provocative pose. 'Your gorgon's trying to stop me coming in, Luke, but you can spare me five minutes, can't you?'

Kate couldn't hear Luke's reply, but Helen gave another throaty laugh and pushed the door to behind her triumphantly.

Kate was left staring at the blank door, shaken by a gust of contradictory feelings; dislike, envy, disgust. There she had been, marvelling at how hard and invulnerable he seemed, and all it took was a pair of long legs and few provocative poses and he was as gullible as any other man!

Well, it was none of her business, of course. Kate resumed typing angrily. If Luke was fool enough to take up with a girl he already had good reason to distrust, that was his look-out.

But she wished he weren't. She didn't mind his being rude, or aggressive, or even unpleasant, but she didn't like his being stupid.

Kate made four mistakes in the letter she was typing before she gave up and stalked along to the coffee machine to work off her bad temper. Returning to her desk, she ripped the paper out of the printer and started afresh.

She was not going to get involved with Luke's business.

She was not going to care if he wanted to make a fool of himself.

She was sensible, practical, capable Kate.

By the time the door reopened she had talked herself into believing it, and was absorbed in typing, the epitome of a discreet, efficient secretary.

Luke ignored her as he walked with Helen to the outer door. 'See you later, then,' he said, letting his hand slide down the shimmering fall of hair.

'I'll be waiting.' Helen lifted her face, and he kissed her on the lips before patting her on the bottom as she left with evident reluctance.

He turned back to the office. Kate's face was mask-like as she picked up a folder from the desk.

'Here are those letters for signature.'

For once, Luke looked taken aback. 'You've finished them already?'

'Of course.' Kate met his eyes blandly. 'You said you wanted them urgently, and I knew how busy you were this morning.'

Luke's slate-grey eyes narrowed as he took the folder from her, but he made no comment at her sly dig at the time he had spent with Helen.

'I'm going to finish that report,' he grunted. 'I don't want to be disturbed.'

'By anyone?' asked Kate, all innocence.

'By anyone!' he snapped, striding over to his office. He banged the door shut behind him, but a few moments later it reopened.

'Kate?'

'Yes?'

'Get me some coffee, will you?' He half closed the door again, then thought better of it, and stuck his head round once more. 'Please!'

It didn't take Kate long to fall into a routine. Every morning she would arrive promptly at nine o'clock, but Luke was always there before her. Sometimes she wondered if he ever went home.

As he had predicted, Luke was a difficult man to work for. He threw huge amounts of work at her and set impossible deadlines, expected her to have acquired an encyclopaedic knowledge of the company on her first day, and snapped if she proved less than a mind-reader. She was rarely able to leave on time and soon learnt not to expect any appreciation from Luke.

In spite of it all, Kate was content. She might deplore Luke's manners, but she couldn't help being impressed by his undoubted abilities. He had an immense capacity for work, and could absorb the most technical of reports with startling speed. A shrewd financial brain combined with ruthless drive had made him one of the most successful men in his field, and, while he might not be loved by his staff, he was universally respected.

Kate dealt with all the work quietly, efficiently and with a complete lack of fuss that gradually earnt a grudging respect from Luke. She never flapped, or complained, or bothered him with silly questions, and their battles were limited to her insistence on courtesy. Luke grumbled about having to say please and thank you the whole time, but usually gave in to Kate in the end.

'You obviously don't dislike him as much as you said you did,' Serena said. She and Kate were sitting in a wine-bar, making the most of the free peanuts.

'No-o.' Kate hesitated. 'He hasn't done anything to make me like him particularly, but I suppose we get on quite well when he's not shouting at me and I'm not ticking him off about his manners.'

'Don't get on too well. He might recognise you!'

Kate shook her head. 'I'm just his secretary,' she said with an unconsciously wistful smile. 'Luke's single-minded in the office. As long as I get through all the work, he wouldn't notice if I did the dance of the seven veils on his desk—he'd just tell me not to mess up his papers!'

'He sounds awful,' Serena said frankly, pinching the last peanut. 'I don't know why you put up with him.'

'He's not that bad,' Kate said, instantly on the defensive. 'He'll talk to me about work and let me make my own comments and suggestions.'

'Big of him!'

'It's more than he does with most people. He was always a loner, and now he's even more so. He keeps people at a distance. I made him laugh the other day, and I felt as if I'd just conquered Everest!'

'Why, what did he do?'

'Nothing. He just laughed. I've seen him smile, of course, but it's usually more of a sneer. This was a proper laugh...' Kate trailed off. It was impossible to explain to Serena the sheer unexpectedness of seeing Luke throw back his head and laugh. All she had done was make a dry comment about a newspaper headline, and suddenly it had been as if a complete stranger stood before her, his face alight with humour, and she had been shaken by the rush of triumphant warmth she had felt. She had made him laugh! She had got through that iron wall of indifference, and without even trying.

'He's much nicer when he laughs,' she finished lamely.

'Kate!' Serena put down her wine glass and looked at Kate with foreboding. 'You're not—you're *not*—thinking of doing anything silly like falling for Luke, are you?'

Falling for Luke? Kate shrugged off a small shiver of memory.

'Of course not,' she said crisply. She took a sip of her wine and avoided Serena's accusing eyes. 'You ought to know me better than that, Serena! I'll admit that I like him more than I expected, but I'm far too sensible to fall for a man like Luke. That would be asking for trouble!'

CHAPTER FOUR

KATE went into work the following Monday to find Luke sitting on the edge of her desk, flicking through the diary.

'Good morning,' she said, hanging up her coat and wishing she could get Serena's ridiculous suggestion out of her mind. She felt cross at the very thought. She knew enough about Luke to be under no illusions about him, and there was no danger whatsoever of her falling for him. The whole idea was absurd! So absurd that it had kept her awake at nights. After two restless nights she felt grouchy and irritable and on edge.

Luke had merely grunted in response to her greeting as he compared the desk diary with the slim leather one he carried in his pocket.

'I said, good morning!' Kate reminded him, and he looked up with an exasperated sigh.

'Oh, very well...good morning, Kate.' He eyed her sardonically. 'Is that sufficient, or do I need to say anything else?'

'You could ask me if I had a nice weekend,' Kate suggested, refusing to be intimidated by his sarcasm.

'Did you have a nice weekend?'

'Yes, thank you. And you?'

'Not particularly,' he snapped. 'Now that we've done the social bit, can we get on with some work? We're going to Paris tomorrow.' He pushed the diary across the desk towards her. 'Just for one night. Get on to the travel agents and book a hotel and two flights—first class.'

'When you say "we", does that include me?' Kate asked carefully.

'As there are just two of us in the room, I'd have thought that was obvious. Why, is there a problem?'

'It's rather short notice.'

'So?'

'I might have something planned,' she pointed out, searching in her bag for her own diary.

'You'll just have to cancel it,' Luke said unsympathetically. 'This is important. And that reminds me, don't book any appointments for this afternoon.'

'Are you going to be out?'

'*We* are going to be out,' he corrected her. 'I'm taking you to get your hair cut.'

Kate had been making neat notes in the diary, but her head jerked up at that. 'I don't need to have my hair cut!'

'Yes, you do. It's important to give our clients the right impression of LPM, and I don't want you turning up in Paris looking like that.'

'Looking like *what*?' Kate's voice was deceptively mild but her eyes held a glitter of frost.

Luke hunched his shoulders irritably. 'You look so bloody prim and proper with your hair tied back like that and those sensible suits of yours. It's like having a governess instead of a secretary!'

'I suppose I should be flattered that you even notice what I wear,' Kate snapped back, angry and more than a little hurt. 'I'd always thought that as long as I typed your letters and answered your phone I could be dressed in rags for all you would care!'

'There's no need to get hysterical,' Luke said. He stood up and tucked his diary back into the inside pocket of his jacket.

The lack of interest in the gesture infuriated Kate. 'I am *not* hysterical!' she said through gritted teeth. 'Why do men always say that as soon as women dare to answer back?'

'If that were the case I'd be permanently accusing you of being hysterical,' Luke pointed out. 'Anyway, what are you getting so het up about? I only made a simple comment about your appearance.'

'Oh, it was a simple comment, was it? I don't suppose it occurred to you that I might not like being accused of being prim and proper, or looking like a governess? Does it even occur to you that I'm a human being and not just another piece of office machinery?'

Luke glowered. 'For heaven's sake, stop over-reacting!'

'No wonder your secretaries keep leaving you!' Kate was searching for a pen, banging papers up and down on her desk furiously. 'You have no consideration for other people's feelings at all!'

'I'm not in the business of worrying about feelings,' Luke said coldly. 'As far as I'm con-cerned, you're here to do a job, and part of that job involves projecting the right image of the company. Now, if you want to look like some uptight spinster when you're in London, that's fine, but this meeting tomorrow is my big chance to break into the European market, and I'm not going to blow it just because you can't be bothered to make the right impression!'

'What's wrong with what I've got on?' Kate demanded, gesturing down at her Prince of Wales check. 'It's smart, and it's suitable. What more do you want?'

'I want some style!' Luke said, exasperated. 'There's nothing wrong with that suit, but it doesn't do anything for you, and nor does your hairstyle. That's all I'm saying.'

'All you're saying is that you don't mind having an efficient secretary, but you'd really rather I looked completely different!'

Luke's mouth was set in an angry line. 'If you're going to be unreasonable, Kate, I'm not going to bother arguing with you!'

'Me, unreasonable?' Kate pushed back her chair and leapt to her feet. Luke's comments had caught her on the raw and she was angrier than she had ever been, certainly too angry to consider what she was saying. 'You're a fine one to talk! You've got a nerve, going on about the impression you're afraid I'll make in Paris when you're the one who hasn't the first idea of how to behave!'

The black look had descended on Luke's face. 'I should be careful what you say to me, Kate,' he warned. 'You're not the only girl in the world who can speak French.'

'I'm probably the only one who would put up with your rudeness!' Kate retorted. 'You treat everyone here like your slaves. Do this, do that, dress like this, cut your hair like that! Well, I'm your secretary, not your slave, and I'm not going to change my image just to suit you!'

'Don't push me too far, Kate,' Luke ground out, 'or you won't be my secretary much longer!'

'Fine!' Incandescent with rage, Kate snatched up her bag and marched over to the coatstand.

'Where do you think you're going?'

'Where do you think?' Kate said, dragging on her coat. 'I'm going to find an employer who'll appreciate the skills I have to offer and who doesn't care if he has to put up with some grotesque frump sitting in the front office!'

Her hand was at the door and she had half opened it when Luke strode over and pushed it firmly shut. 'I didn't say that!'

He was standing very close to her. Kate dropped her hand from the door-handle but stood her ground. 'It sounded like that to me!' she said.

Luke stared down at her. Her face was bright with anger, her eyes glittering and her chin set defiantly.

'Oh, hell!' He raked his fingers through his dark hair and sighed. 'Look, I'm sorry. I shouldn't have spoken to you like that. I had rather a fraught weekend, and I was taking my bad temper out on you. I'm sorry.'

Kate was so surprised to hear him apologise that she could only look uncertainly up into his face.

'I do appreciate you,' he went on. 'You're the best secretary I've ever had.' And then, unfairly, he smiled. 'Honestly!'

Kate's defences were no proof against a smile like that. She took a step back. Really, it was just a smile, just a crease in his cheek, a glimpse of teeth, a rare glimmer of warmth in his eyes. It was nothing to get excited about. There was absolutely no reason for her anger to melt like butter in a hot pan.

She tried to cling on to the last remnants of fury, but it was hopeless, and Luke must have read it in her face. 'Come on,' he said. 'Let's sit down and discuss this sensibly.'

Kate let him help her off with her coat and hang it back on the stand. She stood, remembering the way she had spoken to him and feeling foolish. What had got into her?

Luke propelled her into his office and sat her down on one of the soft leather chairs. 'I'll get some coffee,' he said.

Taken aback by such unexpected treatment, Kate perched uncomfortably on the edge of the chair and accepted the proffered cup gingerly. She wasn't at all sure how to deal with Luke's being nice like this!

'Now,' said Luke, hitching up his trousers and sitting down opposite her, 'can we start again?'

'I'm sorry. I was being stupid,' Kate muttered.

'I think we were both being unreasonable. Your weekend obviously wasn't any better than mine!' Luke stirred his coffee thoughtfully. 'I wasn't lying when I said you were the best secretary I'd ever had. It makes a real difference to me to have someone I can chuck work at and know it will get done properly. I don't need to tell you anything twice. I don't need to send letters back to be retyped. I don't need to worry in case I haven't got all the documents for a meeting. I can *trust* you. I appreciate all of that, believe me.' He paused. 'Perhaps I should have told you this before, but...well, I get absorbed in what I'm doing. I'm not the easiest of men to work for, I know.'

'You did warn me.' Kate had managed to pull herself together and was making an effort to sound brisk and practical. 'I really shouldn't complain.'

Luke looked up from his coffee with a swift smile of such dangerous charm that Kate, in spite of a valiant attempt not to succumb, smiled back.

He had always had a treacherous charm, she remembered, even as she smiled, all the more effective for being so rarely used. She wanted to resist, but there was a warm glow inside her, a tug of response to the light in his blue-grey eyes.

'Shall we just agree that you're the best of secretaries, and I'm the rudest man in the world, and not agonise about it any more?' Luke suggested, and when Kate nodded he leant forward and stretched out his hand. 'Let's shake on it.'

Almost reluctantly Kate took his hand. Long, strong fingers closed around hers in a firm grip, and she felt something clench at the base of her spine.

'That just means that you can go back to being rude while I'll go back to being efficient,' she said as lightly as she could.

'I expect we will, but I promise to try harder, if you'll stay as my secretary.' He released her hand and sat back. 'Will you?'

Kate relented. 'Of course.'

'Good.' Luke eyed her speculatively. 'And you'll let me buy you some new clothes?'

'I thought you wanted me to get a haircut!'

'That too.' Having seen how easily she succumbed to his devastating charm, Luke was losing no opportunity to make the most of it, Kate thought almost resentfully. 'Look, you're important to this Paris trip. I'm relying on you to interpret, so they'll be concentrating on you. I just think it would help LPM's cause if you projected a different sort of image.'

Kate could see that she was being outmanoeuvred. 'If you think it's that necessary I'll buy some new clothes myself,' she tried, but he shook his head.

'No, this is to be at my expense.'

'But I really can't let you buy clothes for me!'

'Why not?'

'Well . . . it's too personal.'

'If it bothers you that much, think of it as a kind of uniform,' Luke said, an edge of impatience creeping back into his voice, much to Kate's amusement. He had obviously been nice for long enough.

Realising that there was no point in arguing further at this stage, she stood up and gathered together the cups.

'I'll go shopping this afternoon,' she promised.

It was a busy morning, and Kate was glad of the hectic pace to keep her mind occupied. She didn't want to think about what Luke had said. Prim and proper. Uptight spinster. Was that how he saw her? Was that how she *was*?

She had spent all weekend telling herself how indifferent she was to Luke, only to lose control completely as soon as he criticised her. Some indifference! It would have been far more dignified to have reacted with cool unconcern, instead of shouting like that and then letting herself be won over by a simple smile. Really, it was pathetic!

Kate had resolved to go out and buy a token dress to keep Luke satisfied but she had reckoned without his insisting on accompanying her. He caught her trying to slip out of the office unnoticed, and took her arm in a firm grasp.

'There's really no need for you to go with me,' she protested, propelled despite herself along the pavement by his hand beneath her elbow. 'You must have lots to do this afternoon.'

Luke's smile was almost malicious as he glanced down at her. 'I'm a successful businessman, and that means finding time for the things that matter. I like to keep a close eye on expenditure and select my investments very care-

fully! Left to yourself, Kate, I have no doubt you
would buy yourself some more neat, practical
suits, and that's not what I have in mind at all!'

Five minutes' walk took them to the centre of
Knightsbridge, crowded with shoppers in spite of
the cold February day. Luke swept Kate through
the throng and into a small shop tucked away in
one of the back streets behind Harrods. It was
discreetly lit, with thick carpets and an expens-
ively perfumed air. Inside there were few clothes
on display, but, when Luke had explained what
he wanted to the alarmingly well-dressed sales
staff, a seemingly inexhaustible supply was
produced out of nowhere.

Luke sat on a spindly chair with his arms
crossed as different outfits were held up against
an uncomfortable Kate, nodding abruptly or dismissing them with a wave of his hand.

'She needs autumn colours,' he said as an assistant proffered a bright turquoise dress. 'That's
too hard for her.' Kate eyed it wistfully as it was
whisked out of sight. 'Look,' he went on, picking
up a soft tan skirt that was draped over a sofa
and holding it impersonally against her. 'This is
what she needs—soft lines, earthy colours that
reflect her personality.'

Kate was scarlet with embarrassment, but
neither Luke nor the saleswomen took any notice.
They carried on talking over her as if she were
no more than a dummy, matching shoes with bags

and holding up scarves and belts that appeared out of bottomless drawers.

'Relax!' Luke ordered as Kate shifted uncomfortably yet again. 'I thought you Frenchwomen were supposed to take an interest in clothes.'

'I think I must take after my father,' Kate said glumly. 'My mother and sister can shop till they drop, but I've never been able to get that excited about it.'

'It shows,' Luke said caustically. 'Now, go and try that lot on and look as if you're enjoying yourself!'

The pile was borne off to the fitting-room, while Luke took a mobile telephone out of his briefcase and dialled a number, jabbing at the buttons with characteristic aggression. Kate heard him booking a table for two for dinner that night, and wondered whom he was taking out. Helen Slayne? Or was she the reason for his fraught weekend?

The thought of Helen's vibrant beauty made her study her reflection in the fitting-room a little forlornly. No amount of expensive clothes would give her that kind of glamour.

'Come out and let me have a look,' Luke commanded from the other room.

With a sigh Kate tucked in the olive-green shirt and did up the zip on the skirt. The suede was soft and luxurious, and she smoothed it with her hands as she pulled aside the curtain and presented herself for Luke's inspection.

He walked round her, studying each outfit so dispassionately that Kate's tawny eyes began to snap with golden lights. It was humiliating, standing here, being inspected. She was burningly aware of Luke's eyes on her body—not that he seemed to notice it. She might as well have been made of plastic as he prowled around her, a dark, powerful presence, impossible to ignore.

By the time Kate emerged from the fitting-room, laden with outfits and dressed in her own clothes once more, she was tight-lipped but determined not to get involved in another scene.

Luke was talking into his phone again. 'Helen? It's Luke. Just to say that I won't be able to make it tonight after all... What's that? That's too bad,' he said curtly. 'I've got an important business meeting tonight.' He switched off the phone and banged the aerial back with the flat of his hand as he turned to look at Kate. 'Do they fit?'

'Yes, but——'

'We'll take them all.'

He handed a credit card to a beaming assistant, who hastened to relieve Kate of her burden. 'Now for the hair.'

Kate maintained a frosty silence as Luke led her through what seemed an unnecessarily tortuous route to the hairdressers'. For someone who had a limousine and driver at his disposal, he was far too ready to walk, she thought as she struggled to keep up with his long, decisive stride.

It was a dull, cold day, and Kate wrapped her coat about her against the wind, thinking longingly of the warm, comfortable Mercedes which had been summoned to collect all the bags from the shop and deliver them to Kate's flat later. Luke had flatly refused to wait for it to give them a lift.

'There's no point in sitting around waiting for the car when it's just as quick to walk. Now, hurry up, Kate, or we'll be late.'

The Cadogan Salon was in a quiet street not far from the King's Road. Kate eyed its green awning uneasily, but once inside she was taken into friendly but capable hands.

'I want you to cut it short,' Luke instructed, holding his hand just below Kate's jawline. 'About here. And do anything else you think necessary. I want her to look smart and stylish.' He turned back to Kate. 'I'm going back to the office now. Take a taxi home when they've finished with you here, and be ready for me to pick you up at half-past seven.'

Kate let herself be helped into a gown to protect her suit. 'But I thought you had an important business meeting?'

'I have. I'm taking you out to dinner.'

She stared at him as she tied the belt automatically. 'Me? Why?'

'I want to discuss the Paris trip with you, since we haven't had an opportunity this afternoon,' Luke said briskly. 'And don't try and pretend you're busy. You're the sensible sort of girl who would spend the evening before a trip getting herself organised and making sure you got to bed early, so if you *had* had any plans I'm quite sure you would have cancelled them. Or am I wrong? Is there more behind that demure exterior than meets the eye? Is there a queue of palpitating lovers waiting to take you out tonight?'

His mockery was obvious, and Kate's chin tilted with stiffened pride. 'No, the palpitating lovers were last night.'

There was a brief flash of admiration in Luke's eyes. 'Good,' he said. 'In that case, I'll see you later.' He pulled his diary out of his inside pocket. 'Remind me of your address.'

'It's all right,' Kate said quickly, remembering the photographs of her parents and of the manor in her sitting-room. She didn't want to run the risk of Luke's coming in and recognising them. 'Why don't I just meet you at the restaurant?'

Luke hesitated, then nodded. 'All right,' he said, giving her the name of the restaurant. 'I'll see you there about eight. Wear that green dress I picked out, and don't be late!'

He turned and walked out without more ado, leaving Kate in a state of simmering exasperation at his abrupt orders. So much for his making an effort to be more polite!

Resigned to her fate, she let herself be led off to have her hair washed.

Two hours later she sat in front of the mirror and stared at her own reflection. She had been determined to dislike the way she was to be changed on Luke Hardman's instructions, but now she was taken aback by what she saw. Was that girl in the mirror really her?

The hair which had always been so soberly brown had been cunningly highlighted so that it gleamed as she turned her head—copper, bronze, gold. Then they had taken ruthless scissors to it and, released of its weight, it bounced exuberantly about her face in soft, natural waves, and threw into relief the fine cheekbones, the clear, luminous skin and the long, graceful line of her throat.

'It suits you,' Susan reassured her, mistaking Kate's silence for disappointment. She drew the brush through a wing of burnished hair and let it swing softly forward again.

It did more than suit her. It transformed her. Kate turned her head this way and that, watching her profile out of the corner of her eye, a little annoyed that Luke had been proved so right and almost alarmed at how different she looked. How would she ever be able to live up to such a glamorously vibrant image?

The bright new hair blew about her face as she stood on the King's Road and waved down a taxi. She wondered what Luke would think. It was just like him to bully her into a complete change of appearance! Now she was unsettled, unsure of herself and confused about Luke. Just when she had decided to like him, he was arrogant and unpleasant, and then, as if that weren't enough, he confused her further with a quite unexpected charm. Now she didn't know what she felt!

CHAPTER FIVE

A SUBDUED murmur of voices and the discreet chink of china greeted Kate as she stepped through the door and surrendered her coat to a silently efficient waiter. She felt vulnerable without its protection, and smoothed down her dress nervously.

It was very plain, a deep dark jade, with a wide V neck and arms demurely covered with long, tight sleeves. Otherwise the design was of classic simplicity, the skirt falling from a tailored bodice in soft folds of the finest wool.

It was a dress designed to flatter the wearer rather than itself. Kate had deliberately tried to underplay the effect by not wearing any jewellery, but she was still very aware of the sensuous feel of the soft material against her skin, of the way the stark design emphasised the swell of her breast and the pure sweep of throat and shoulder.

She was still unused to the feel of her hair and she touched it self-consciously as she followed the waiter across the room to where Luke was sitting.

He was studying a wine list with ferocious concentration, dark brows drawn together and lean jaw set, unaware of her approach. His expression was dauntingly grim; he looked like a man who had relied on himself for so long that he had forgotten that others could offer warmth and comfort, and Kate, who had been feeling edgy and resentful of the way he had cast her into confusion, found herself swept by a contrary rush of tenderness so unexpected that she faltered.

He looked up just then and saw her. At first incurious, impatient at his having his concentration broken, his gaze sharpened suddenly as he recognised his quiet, efficient secretary in the woman walking towards him.

Kate wished she weren't so conscious of the subtly alluring sway of the skirt as she moved. She had never been so aware of her own body. She could feel Luke's eyes on her slender curves and longed for her coat, a cardigan, *anything* to wrap around her defensively.

Luke was still holding the wine list. He laid it down very slowly as she came up to the table and then, as if suddenly aware of the waiter's surprised look, rose hastily to his feet.

To Kate's relief, his eyes had left her body and rested on her face, as if he was still having trouble convincing himself that it was really her. She wished he would say something to break the silence, which threatened to become awkward.

Instead, he glanced down at his watch.

'I'm not late!' Kate found herself saying instinctively.

Her sharpness seemed to break the spell, and a more familiar look of impatience closed over his face. 'I didn't say you were.'

'You didn't need to. You just looked at your watch in that very pointed way!'

Kate allowed the waiter to pull out her chair and sat down, ruffled as much by the look that had been in Luke's eyes as she had walked towards him as by her uncharacteristic self-consciousness and the awful realisation that she had hoped he would do more than think about the time.

A half-smile twisted Luke's mouth. 'I was playing for time. I wasn't quite sure it was you until you snapped at me like that!'

Kate's lips tightened. She shook the starched linen napkin out with a pointed flick of her wrists. 'Of course it was me. A haircut doesn't change you that much!'

'Evidently not.' Luke's voice was dry and Kate flushed slightly. He obviously thought she was being shrewish. She must pull herself together.

'The hair's a great improvement,' he went on. 'I told you it would look better short.'

Hardly an effusive compliment! 'Thank you,' Kate said crisply, determined not to let him guess that she was disappointed by his lack of interest.

There was a short pause. Luke looked as if he was about to say something, then changed his mind.

'I've ordered for you,' he said eventually, picking up the wine list once more. 'I thought it would be easier.'

'I'm perfectly capable of choosing my own meal, thank you,' Kate said frostily. 'I have been to a restaurant before, and I won't need the menu translated!'

Luke frowned, but he handed her the menu that lay by his plate with an irritable shrug. 'Have it your own way.'

Kate opened the menu and studied it with spurious interest. She didn't really care what she ate, but it seemed important to keep some control to herself. Luke had ordered her about enough for one day!

Peeping over the top of the menu, she saw that he was intent on the wine list. In dinner-jacket and bow-tie, he looked darkly, dourly attractive. The subdued lighting softened his features, but, when he looked up suddenly and met her gaze over the leather-bound lists, the slate eyes were as penetrating as ever.

Kate dropped her eyes hastily back to the menu.

'Have you decided yet?' Luke asked in a voice of long suffering as a waiter appeared at his elbow.

'I'll have the salmon and sole roulade, and then the magret de canard.' She closed the menu with a defiant snap.

'Sure?'

'Yes, thank you.'

'I was thinking of a Sauvignon to start with, and then a Château d'Yquem,' Luke said with heavy irony. 'Is that acceptable, or would you like to choose the wine too?'

'No, that sounds fine,' Kate said primly, folding her hands in her lap and refusing to rise to the bait.

Luke turned to the waiter. 'We'll have the salmon and sole, and then the duck—as I ordered previously.' When he had ordered the wine he turned back to meet Kate's accusing gaze. 'What's the matter?'

'Why didn't you tell me what you'd ordered?'

'What, and have you choose something different, just to be difficult? I chose what I thought you'd like. What's wrong with that?'

'I've got a mind of my own,' Kate said with a touch of sullenness.

'I'm well aware of that, Kate!'

'You'd never guess it the way you've been treating me today!'

'What do you mean by that?'

'You choose my hairstyle, my clothes, my meal... I might as well be a plastic dummy sitting here!'

'Don't be ridiculous!' Luke said crossly. 'I thought we went through all that this morning?'

'We agreed that you appreciated my work and that you'd make more effort to be pleasant.'

'I have!'

'I don't call it pleasant to make someone parade in front of you while you walk round them and criticise as if they were in some kind of cattle market!'

'So that's why you were in such a bad mood all afternoon,' Luke said, inspecting the bottle of wine presented by the waiter. He waited until a small amount had been poured into his glass, then took a sip, and nodded. 'Most women would have enjoyed having an afternoon at the hair-dressers', not to mention a free wardrobe.'

Kate waited until the waiter had finished pouring the wine. 'I'm not most women,' she pointed out tartly as he left the bottle on the table and disappeared discreetly. 'I'm me, and I don't appreciate being treated like . . . like some kind of bimbo!'

To her chagrin, instead of looking contrite, Luke grinned. 'Kate, you're the last person I'd treat as a bimbo!'

She wished he wouldn't smile like that. Kate seized her glass and took a gulp of wine, trying to keep her eyes off the heart-wrenching lift of his mouth.

'As far as I'm concerned,' Luke said, 'you're a sensible and intelligent woman, and a damn sight too valuable to me to start treating like a sex object! I can't tell you what a relief it is to find a woman prepared to keep a relationship on a strictly business footing, and who doesn't expect to be showered with compliments!'

'One every now and then wouldn't go amiss!'

'I would have said that you look wonderful in that dress, but you'd probably just have accused me of being sexist!' For a moment their eyes clashed, and then Luke smiled ruefully. 'I'm sorry,' he apologised. 'It's just a bit of a shock to find my prim and proper secretary transformed so suddenly into something quite different!' He reached over and touched her hand briefly. 'You look beautiful tonight, Kate. Is that better?'

Kate was glad of the dim light that disguised the deep flush that swept up her throat. She withdrew her hand hastily, shaken by the way her heart had jolted at his touch.

'I was only joking,' she muttered. 'Sensible and intelligent were enough of a compliment!'

'Were they? I don't know of any other woman who would have been satisfied with that!'

'Ah, but as far as you're concerned I'm not a woman,' Kate said drily. 'I'm your secretary.'

Luke picked up his glass and looked at her over the rim, an enigmatic expression in his eyes.

'When you look the way you do tonight it's hard to remember.'

Kate felt as if she had stepped suddenly on to uncertain ground, and she took a hasty sip of wine while she tried desperately to think of a way to bring the conversation back to safe, familiar territory. She was tense, flustered by the warmth in his voice.

'You said you wanted to talk to me about the trip to Paris,' she reminded him, wondering if her voice sounded that high and unnatural to him too. 'Whom exactly are we going to meet?'

She avoided looking directly at him, certain that he would read the silly, girlish flutterings of her heart in her eyes. She wasn't sixteen now, she chided herself. She was a grown woman, too sensible to misinterpret the most casual of compliments, the briefest of touches. This was a business dinner, that was all. True, Luke was being pleasant, but it really shouldn't set her heart pounding like this...

Luke gave her a quick, keen look, but answered her readily enough. 'Philippe Robard and his grandson, who's also a director of the company. Robard owns the Oasis chain of hotels—you must have heard of them when you were in France?'

When Kate nodded he went on, 'He's expanding fast, with an eye to the UK in particular. You probably know that his speciality is buying up old buildings—mostly run-down châteaux—

and transforming them into five-star hotels. Everything top quality, of course, but with an eye to retaining the original character of the building as far as possible.'

He fiddled absently with his knife. 'Robard's been extraordinarily successful so far, but he needs to be careful not to lose quality control as he expands. He's a hotelier, not an engineer.'

'And that's where we come in?' Kate was concentrating fiercely on what he was saying to take her mind off its sudden obsession with his mouth.

'Exactly. I'm offering him a complete consultancy service on the construction front, leaving him free to concentrate on running the hotels. That's why it's so important that we give him the right impression tomorrow. He needs to feel that we embody the qualities he's looking for in his buildings: style, efficiency, quality.'

Kate hailed the arrival of the waiter with the first course with relief. Now she would be able to look at her plate. 'He can get all that from a French firm, can't he?' she said vaguely, picking up her knife and fork.

'Yes, but remember he wants to get a foothold in the UK as much as I want to get one in France.' Luke seemed more interested in his business than in his food. 'We've got a good international reputation outside Europe, and you, Kate, are going to give us our European flavour.'

'I see.' Kate's eyes were lowered to her plate, and a wing of hair shone in the reflected light. 'What exactly do you want me to do?'

'You'll be there as my assistant, and, obviously, to help out with any language problems. I expect you to impress them with your efficiency and the charm which I know very well you possess, even if you don't waste any of it on me!'

Kate looked up in astonishment and her eyes, huge and dark, caught the gleam of gold from a candle near by. She put her knife and fork down slowly. 'What on earth do you mean?'

It was Luke's turn to concentrate on his dinner. 'I've seen the way you talk to people in the office. They all like you. I'm sick of my directors telling me how charming you are! All I ever get from you is disapproval or a lecture about my manners, or lack of them.'

There was a strange note in his voice, and Kate bit her lip. She could almost swear he was hurt!

'That's not fair,' she protested. 'I'm perfectly nice to you sometimes.'

Luke leant over to refill her wine glass, and then his own. 'Only sometimes!' he said, but she was relieved to see a glint of amusement in his eyes. 'The trouble with you, Kate, is that you're very honest—sometimes uncomfortably so. I'm not used to that. I learnt early on not to expect too much honesty from women.'

Bitterness shadowed his voice and Kate wondered if he was remembering Helen. Was she being any more honest than Helen in not admitting that she had met Luke before? she wondered guiltily.

On an impulse she opened her mouth to tell him, but then the waiter was beside them, checking their glasses, offering them another roll, and by the time he had gone the moment had passed and Luke had changed the subject.

'I suppose going to Paris tomorrow will be like going home for you?'

'In a way,' she said, not sorry to let go of the opportunity to tell Luke the truth. It would only have embarrassed them both. 'It's funny, all the time I was in France I thought about coming back to England, and now I'm here I think about France just as nostalgically. Having dual nationality makes you a little schizophrenic!'

'I never think of you as being French,' Luke said thoughtfully. 'You always seem so cool and English.'

'I take after my father.'

'What was he like?'

Kate wondered what Luke would say if she told him that he knew perfectly well. He had always despised her father, she remembered, had thought of him as stuffy and snobbish. He hadn't known how kind and generous her father could be to those he loved.

'He was rather cool and English too,' she said lightly.

There was a lurking smile about Luke's mouth. 'He sounds all right.'

For one dizzy moment time seemed to telescope, and Kate found herself wishing desperately that her father could have known this new Luke.

'So you don't regret coming back to England?'

'No.' Kate shook her head, feeling the shining softness bounce against her cheek. 'I would have come back before, but my mother is...well, she's very gay and very charming, but hopelessly impractical! After my father died and we went to France it somehow seemed natural that I would look after things like money. Veronique, my half-sister, was married by then, but I was always more sensible than her anyway, even as a child.' She sighed.

'What's wrong with being sensible?'

'Nothing. It's just that sometimes I wonder what would have happened if I'd gone through a rebellious stage. I might have had more fun.'

'Kicking the system? I did all that,' Luke said.

'Oh, I——' Kate stopped. She had been about to say 'I know'. 'I can imagine,' she said after an infinitesimal pause.

Luke didn't seem to have noticed. 'I thought I was having fun at the time, but, looking back,

I think I was just unhappy.' He gave a careless shrug, but Kate felt suddenly ashamed.

It had never occurred to her before that the cold recklessness of Luke's youth had been due to unhappiness. It was well-known in the village that his mother had left years before, and since then he had lived alone with his father, an eccentric and rather reclusive man. No, his memories of Chittingdene would probably not be happy ones. She was glad she hadn't mentioned the past. Luke gave the impression of a man who had put it firmly behind him.

'How is your mother managing without you now?' he was asking.

'She got married again a few months ago.' Kate took a sip of wine. 'Thierry is far more capable than I am of looking after my mother, and he can afford to spoil her, but...'

'But you don't like him?'

'No. I've tried, but we just don't get on. Oh, it was all very polite, but somehow that made it even worse. When my sister sent Solange to school here it was an ideal excuse to leave without hurting my mother's feelings...' Kate trailed off. She hadn't meant to tell Luke all this, but somehow it had all come out. 'They'll be far better off without me cramping their style,' she finished briskly. 'My mother's a great party-goer, and always beautifully dressed. I'm afraid I didn't inherit any of her sense of style! She certainly looks far too young to have a daughter as old as me!'

'She sounds rather like someone I used to know, or at least know of. What was her name, now?' Luke's eyes narrowed in an effort of memory. 'Well, it doesn't matter what her name was, but she was a Frenchwoman too—far too glamorous and racy for Chittingdene!'

Kate put her fork down on the plate rather unsteadily. 'Chittingdene?'

'The village where I grew up,' Luke explained. 'It's a sleepy little place buried in Somerset. I haven't been there for years. Couldn't wait to leave.' He stared into his wine. 'It's strange, I haven't thought of Chittingdene in years. I certainly haven't thought of Mrs... what *was* her name, now?'

'How did you get into project management?' Kate asked quickly, anxious to divert his mind from the past. She was surprised that he remembered her mother, who had always found village life much too staid and had spent as much time as possible in France.

Luke was talking, but her mind kept veering back to the past, comparing the rebellious youth she had known to the determined man who sat opposite her now, telling her about his struggle to succeed. They were so alike, and yet so different. Or was it just that she had been too young to see him properly before?

'It must have been hard work,' she commented when he looked at her with raised brows, obviously wondering at her silence.

'It was,' Luke said. 'But worth it in the end. I'm a rich man now.'

'I suppose you must be,' Kate said doubtfully, thinking of what a long, lonely slog it must have been.

'You don't sound very sure, Kate,' he said with some amusement. 'No, don't tell me! Money isn't everything?'

'Well, it isn't, is it?'

'Kate, I'm disappointed in you! It's not like you to be trite. I suppose you think I should have acquired a wife and children and a dog to fetch my slippers along the way to make it all worthwhile?'

Kate met his eyes with her clear gaze. He was mocking, but there was an underlying edge of defensiveness in his voice. 'I don't think you *should* have married. I'm just surprised you haven't.'

'I never wanted to get married,' he said shortly. 'I like my women as cynical as I am. That way no one expects anything and no one gets hurt.'

Don't they? Kate thought. What about the boy abandoned by his mother, shrugged aside by Helen Slayne? What about the years of cynicism hardening slowly into bitterness?

'What about you?' Luke asked. 'Why aren't you married? Are you holding out for Mr Right? Or pining for a long-lost love?'

Unbidden, a memory of that long-distant summer's day washed over Kate. The smell of the long grass, the touch of his hands, the taste of his kiss. But that wasn't love, she reminded herself fiercely. That was just an initiation, a glimpse of how things might be.

'I'm not married because nobody has ever asked me to marry him.'

'Nobody's seen the way you look tonight.'

'No,' Kate agreed, hating his casual, meaningless words, her smile brittle. 'You're the first.'

Luke was turning a spoon between his fingers as he watched her, but now he stopped and replaced it deliberately back by his plate. 'I suppose I am,' he said slowly.

An uncomfortable silence fell. Kate gulped at her wine and searched her mind feverishly for a way to steer the conversation back to less personal waters. They were supposed to be talking business. How had they got on to love and marriage?

'Is Monsieur Robard——?'

'Do you know——?'

They both spoke at once, and broke off awkwardly.

'Go on,' Kate said, embarrassed.

'I was just going to ask if you knew Paris well,' Luke said in a stilted tone.

Kate seized on the innocuous topic, and for the rest of the meal kept the conversation cool and impersonal with an effort. Plates appeared and disappeared, glasses were refilled. Kate ate and drank and didn't taste any of it. She talked and talked about business, while her eyes kept sliding away from Luke's. She was agonisingly aware of him. She wished he would stop their determinedly polite conversation. She wished he would be rude, or make her angry, do anything to take her mind off the overwhelming desire to reach over and touch him. She was terrified to look at his face in case she couldn't drag her eyes away from his mouth, so she watched the other diners, and the gleam of cutlery, and his fingers curled around the stem of his glass.

At last it was over. Luke helped Kate into her coat and she shivered at the brush of his fingers.

'I'll get you a taxi,' he said as he opened the door for her. 'I can walk from here.'

'I can easily get a bus,' Kate protested, but Luke ignored her, and they walked down to the corner of the road, not touching.

It had been raining. The pavement gleamed under the street-lights and cars passed them slowly, their tyres swishing on the wet road.

Kate dug her hands firmly into her pockets and stared down the road, willing a familiar yellow light to appear. Luke seemed content to wait in silence, but he was watching her so closely that Kate began to get more and more unnerved.

'Is something the matter?' she asked crossly at last.

'I keep getting this feeling I've met you before,' Luke admitted, almost reluctantly. 'I haven't, have I?'

Kate's pulse leapt and she looked quickly away. 'I think I'd remember you if we had met,' she said, unwilling to tell an outright lie now, but unable to face all the explanations if she admitted the truth.

'I suppose it's because you look so different tonight.' Luke sounded dissatisfied. He stepped up beside her on the kerb, and Kate had to make an effort not to flinch at his nearness. He was looking up and down the road, as if as anxious as she for a taxi.

'I can't get used to you like this,' he went on, glancing down at her. 'I keep noticing things I never noticed about you before...' He trailed off, and Kate had the strangest feeling that he had surprised himself as much as her. 'It really is amazing what a difference a haircut makes.'

There was an odd expression in his eyes. Kate wanted to look away but couldn't. Her heart was lurching and bumping in her chest. 'I hope you think you've got a good return on your investment,' she said bravely.

Unhurriedly Luke reached out and pushed the soft wing of hair away from her face. 'I do,' he said. 'I do indeed.'

Before she knew how it happened his hand had slid under her hair to hold her head still as he bent and kissed her.

Caught unawares, with her hands trapped in her pockets, Kate was helpless to resist. She toppled against his lean, hard strength, felt his arm pull her closer.

Past arrowed into present. Here on this damp winter street, with Luke's lips insistent on hers, Kate might have been standing in that summer wood again. The deep ache of need was the same, the yearning, the heady sense of desire at the taste of his mouth and the firmness of his hand at the nape of her neck.

Kate's response was purely instinctive. Her lips parted and she relaxed into him, submerged by a jumbled tide of intense excitement, lurking guilt and recognition that no one else had ever been able to make her feel this way.

She wanted to free her hands from her pockets, to touch his face and feel his male-rough jaw beneath her fingers, but Luke was lifting his head, lifting a hand, and a black taxi squealed to a halt beside them.

The click of its meter seemed unnaturally loud. Dazed, Kate stared at it as if she had never seen a taxi before. 'Wh-what did you do that for?' she managed.

'Just a wise investor enjoying a little profit,' Luke said. She couldn't read his expression as he turned away to speak to the driver, but then he handed her into the taxi and shut the door on her as if nothing had happened.

'I'll see you at the airport at half-past ten,' was all he said through the window. 'Don't be late.'

CHAPTER SIX

THE terminal was crowded, and Kate didn't see Luke until he appeared suddenly beside the check-in desk. He looked about him impatiently, glancing at his watch and obviously wondering where she was.

It gave Kate a moment to school her features to cool unconcern before she stepped forward to attract his notice.

She had spent a restless night, trying to get Luke's kiss out of her mind, but every time she closed her eyes the scene was replayed with the same vivid thrill of memory: his hands, his mouth, the hard, exciting strength of his body close to hers.

Alone in the darkness, she had found it easy to tell herself that she had merely been caught by surprise. Why else would she have leant into him like that? Why else would her lips have yielded to the warm persuasion of his mouth? Why else would she have kissed him back?

Luke should never have kissed her, Kate had decided, finding it easier to be angry with him than to remember her own abandoned response. The most charitable explanation was that it had

been a whim on his part, quite meaningless. Kate
was determined to treat it the same way. It would
be far less embarrassing for them both if she just
ignored the whole issue.

But now, with the stomach-clenching jolt of
her heart at the sudden sight of him, with the fire
leaping along her pulse, it didn't seem quite so
easy.

No sign of her inner turmoil showed in Kate's
face as she wished Luke a cool good morning.

Luke's eyes were shuttered as he returned her
greeting curtly, and to Kate's relief he was dis-
inclined for conversation as they checked in and
went through Passport Control into the de-
parture lounge. He looked grumpy, and Kate was
glad to take refuge behind an air of brisk
efficiency.

She was wearing one of the outfits Luke had
picked out, a soft tan skirt with a loosely struc-
tured jacket and an ivory silk shirt. The casual
elegance suited her understated looks, but Luke
didn't comment. He had taken some papers out
of his briefcase and was studying them with a
grim face, effectively ignoring her.

Kate eyed him covertly. His brows were drawn
together, his mouth set in an inflexible line. He
looked so hard and forbidding that if it hadn't
been for the way her pulse was beating it would
have been hard to believe that this was the same
man who had kissed her last night.

Did he even remember? Kate wouldn't have put it past him to have put it completely out of his mind as soon as she'd been out of sight. Their first kiss hadn't meant anything to him; why should their second? Unconsciously wistful, Kate's eyes deepened to the colour of honey, and she glanced at him again. If Luke *did* remember kissing her he had obviously decided to ignore it now.

Well, that suited her!

'I suppose you're waiting for me to apologise for kissing you last night,' Luke said abruptly, without looking up from his notes.

Kate, just relaxing into the comfortable certainty that the whole embarrassing episode could safely be forgotten, looked at his bent head with resentment. She should have remembered that it wasn't possible to relax with Luke. He had an uncanny ability to catch her at a disadvantage.

'There's no need to apologise,' she said, proud of her cool manner, but unable to look at him directly. Instead she glanced with studied casualness over at the passengers milling around the duty-free shop. 'I didn't take it seriously.'

He looked up at that. She didn't see him, but she could feel his sharp eyes upon her.

'Oh? And how *did* you take it?'

Why couldn't he just accept the let-out she had given him? Kate thought crossly. It was just like him to be difficult about the whole thing!

'You clearly weren't thinking about what you were doing.'

'How do you work that one out?'

There was the merest suspicion of amusement in his voice and Kate's eyes flickered back to him suspiciously, but he was looking down at his papers again. All she could see were the angular lines of nose and cheek as he scribbled notes.

Her pride rebelling at her being cross-examined by Luke in this embarrassing way while he had half a mind on a quite different subject, Kate spoke more waspishly than she had intended.

'I'd have thought it was obvious. In your book, girl plus dinner plus darkness equals kiss. Unfortunately, you left the fact that I'm your secretary out of the equation.'

'I think I must have forgotten that, under that glamorous new image of yours, a disapproving Kate still lurks,' Luke said with some dryness, making a final note and then slipping his pen into his jacket pocket.

'It's not my new image. It's yours,' Kate pointed out sulkily.

'Oh, I don't know,' Luke said judiciously. He put his papers back into his briefcase and snapped it shut. 'All I did was spot the beautiful, rather sexy woman you could be if only you'd let yourself.'

Kate felt herself grow suddenly hot. She would have given anything to have been able to say something cutting in reply, but could only stare fiercely at the book-stall while she fought down a blush. She wished he wouldn't say things like that. He was so much easier to deal with when he was being downright unpleasant.

'I don't want to be beautiful and sexy,' she said desperately. 'I'm not like that.'

'You were like that when I kissed you last night.'

'You caught me unawares,' Kate defended herself. She drew a deep breath and forced herself to look straight into Luke's slate-grey eyes. '*You* were the one who went on about how grateful you were that our relationship was strictly business, so I'd be grateful if you'd remember that in future. Since we have to work together, it seems only sensible.'

'Very sensible,' Luke mocked. 'I wouldn't expect a sensible secretary like you, Kate, to suggest anything else!' He glanced up at the flight monitor and, much to Kate's relief, got to his feet, putting an end to the discussion. 'Come on, the flight's boarding now.'

Paris was veiled in a typically pale blue-grey light as they took a taxi into the centre from the airport. They were staying at the Paris Oasis on the rue du Faubourg-St-Honoré, the standard-bearer of Philippe Robard's chain of hotels, and Kate was impressed by its understated elegance.

She looked about the magnificent lobby as Luke signed them in with his usual brusque efficiency. If this was Philippe Robard's standard then Luke had been right to insist on a change of image for her!

Luke gave no sign of appreciating the luxurious surroundings. He allowed Kate a bare five minutes to comb her hair before whisking her off to their meeting with Philippe Robard.

'Now, remember,' he said as they waited for the doorman to find them a taxi, 'you're to be pleasant and charming. I don't want to hear you lecturing Robard about his manners!'

'I wouldn't dream of it,' Kate said loftily.

'Oh, wouldn't you?' Luke snorted. 'Just smile and be nice, that's all I ask. Let's have a look at you...' He turned her to face him and subjected her to a critical inspection, from the gleaming hair to the smart new tan shoes. The soft lines of the skirt and jacket gave her an easy elegance, and the warm colours flattered her fine skin and reflected the tawny brown of her eyes.

Kate waited for him to find something to criticise, but he turned abruptly away as the taxi drew up. 'You look all right,' was all he said.

Philippe Robard was a slight man of about sixty with an aloof, patrician face. He greeted them courteously and introduced his son, Xavier, who gazed at Kate with frank admiration as he shook her hand. He was darkly handsome with olive skin and caressing eyes, and Kate could feel Luke stiffen with disapproval. Next to the two stylish Frenchmen, he looked massive and granite-hard.

After the initial exchange of courtesies they soon got down to business. It was a tough meeting, and it was clear that Philippe Robard was quite as shrewd a negotiator as Luke. They spoke in French, which meant that Luke could understand and put across the simple facts, but he left Kate to translate the more complex ideas.

Winning a contract like this was not going to be easy, Kate realised as she explained how LPM worked to Philippe and Xavier. Mindful of what Luke had said, she made a special effort to smile and be charming, until even Philippe's stern features relaxed. Xavier was clearly even more impressed. He kept his warm brown eyes on her face, and smiled charmingly back at her.

Kate was very conscious of Luke sitting beside her. There was a coiled tension about him as he leant forward to show Philippe and Xavier photographs of the better-known projects LPM had completed, and she wondered just how much winning this contract meant to him. He was arguing persuasively, but she knew him well enough by now to be able to tell that he was keeping a simmering anger in check. Kate was mystified. She couldn't imagine what he had to be angry about. The meeting was going well, better even than they had hoped.

Xavier caught her eye and smiled as Luke sat back in his chair, and she smiled politely back. Privately she thought he should be studying Luke's figures instead of hers, but Luke had insisted that she be nice, so she had better not spoil things now. Still wondering about Luke, she glanced at him, only to encounter such a blazing look that her eyes widened in surprise.

Philippe chose that moment to rise. 'I regret that I have another appointment now,' he said in heavily accented English, 'but perhaps we may continue this very interesting discussion this evening?'

'Of course.' Luke got to his feet too. 'I hope that you will both be my guests for dinner?' His glance included Xavier, but without much enthusiasm.

'Miss Finch will be there too?' Xavier asked, with another flashing smile at Kate.

'Naturally,' Luke said curtly.

'In that case, it will be a real pleasure!'

Outside, the street was crowded with shoppers. Luke set off down the pavement, barely waiting to see if Kate was following. His face was set in forbidding lines, his jaw thrust forward angrily.

'The meeting seemed to go quite well,' Kate ventured, hurrying to keep up.

'We haven't got the contract yet,' he pointed out grumpily.

'Well, no, but I think they were impressed.'

'Oh, they were impressed all right, but I suspect it was more by those big smiles of yours than by anything I might have had to say! I'm not denying that I want this contract badly, but there's no need to offer yourself on a plate for it!'

Kate's jaw dropped, and she stopped dead in the middle of the pavement. 'What on earth do you mean?'

'Oh, come on, Kate! All those coquettish looks at Xavier, those little sidelong smiles. I must say, I never suspected you had quite such a talent for flirting!'

'*Flirting*?' It was so unfair that it took Kate a few moments to get her words out. 'I was only being pleasant, as *you* asked—though ordered might be a more accurate word!'

'There's a difference between being pleasant and laying it on with a trowel!'

Kate's eyes were ablaze with gold as she stalked down the pavement. 'Aren't you ever satisfied? You went on and on and *on* about how I had to be charming, so I was. I smiled and was nice, just as you ordered, and now you turn round and accuse me of flirting! I suppose if I hadn't smiled I'd have been deliberately jeopardising your chances?'

'You didn't do all that much for them, sitting there making eyes at that creep Xavier, either!' Luke snapped, striding along beside her. 'God only knows what Robard thought!'

'What should he think? That you had a pleasant and efficient secretary to act as your interpreter, that's all!'

'Yes, one who did her best to distract his son from the details of the proposals! I wouldn't be surprised if Robard thought I'd asked you to do it deliberately because I didn't think the proposal would stand up to much scrutiny. You and Xavier spent so much time smiling at each other that he didn't have a chance to look at the details!'

'He smiled at me, I smiled back! What was I supposed to do, put a bag over my head?'

The tension that had simmered between them all day had flared into anger out of all proportion to what had happened. Kate was beside herself with fury. She had done exactly as Luke had asked, and what thanks did she get? He was totally unreasonable; anyone would think he was jealous, the way he was carrying on! If she had any guts she would tell him just what he could do with his job and get the first train back to Dijon. Let him win his precious contract without her!

Storming onwards, Kate stepped off the pavement without thinking, only to find herself hauled back by an iron hand as a battered Renault shot past with a squeal of tyres, a blast of horn and a rude gesture out of the window.

'For God's sake, look where you're going!' Luke shouted at her. 'You could have been killed!'

Kate struggled to free her arm, but Luke kept a firm hold of it as he looked pointedly each way to check that nothing was coming and then marched her across the road.

'Let go of me!'

'You might at least thank me for saving your life!'

'Quite frankly, I don't feel like thanking you for anything at the moment.' Kate managed to shake her arm free at last. 'In fact, I don't feel like talking to you at all until you're more reasonable.' She turned towards a side-street. 'I'll see you back at the hotel.'

'You're here on business, not pleasure, Kate,' Luke said dangerously. 'That means you don't just flounce off on your own without asking!'

'I'm your secretary, not your slave. I'm entitled to some free time.'

A muscle worked in Luke's jaw. 'Oh, very well, if you must! There's no point in trying to do any work when you're in this kind of mood. Just make sure you're not late, and come back in a better temper!'

He was a fine one to talk about temper, Kate thought savagely as she stalked off. Muttering to herself about Luke, she hardly noticed where she was going until she found herself unexpectedly on boulevard Haussmann. Determined not to go back to the hotel until the last minute, she went into one of the large department stores that lined the street.

She emerged some time later, clutching a large carrier-bag, a defiant glint in her eyes. If Luke thought that she was set on flirting she would show him just what she could do when she tried!

It was dark by the time she got back to the hotel, and the shop windows along the rue du Faubourg-St-Honoré glittered invitingly, each more opulently chic than the last. Kate slowed her steps as she passed, oblivious to the crowds hurrying past her on their way home, her French blood approving the sheer sophistication and style of the displays.

There was no sign of Luke as she collected her key at reception and made her way to her room, but hardly had she put the key in the lock than Luke's door opened, so abruptly that she could almost have suspected that he had been listening out for her.

'About time you turned up! What have you been doing all this time?' he demanded, putting paid to any hope that he might have calmed down enough to apologise.

'Shopping,' Kate said shortly.

'How like a woman! One night away from home, and she has to go to the shops.' Luke glowered and ran his hand through his dark hair. He had evidently been working. His shirt-sleeves were rolled up and his loosened tie hung untidily. 'I hope you're going to be ready in time.'

Kate clenched her teeth. 'Have I ever been late for anything?'

'No, but there's no telling what you might do in the mood you're in!'

'I am *not* in a mood!'

Unexpectedly Luke grinned. 'Oh, yes, you are! I can always tell when you're angry. Those quiet brown eyes of yours fleck with gold and your chin comes up—just the way it is now.'

Kate decided that that wasn't worth answering. 'I shall be ready on time, just as I always am,' she said coldly. 'What time would you like to leave?'

'We arranged to meet them at the restaurant, didn't we? We'd better make sure we're there first. I'll give you a knock at seven—or won't that be enough time for you to get ready?'

There was a malicious glint in his eyes and, although Kate knew that she would have to hurry quite unnecessarily, she would have died rather than ask him to give her a few more minutes.

'Seven o'clock will be fine.'

Kate showered quickly and then sat down in front of the mirror in a towelling robe, her wet hair wrapped in a towel. She had been lured to one of the cosmetic counters in the department store, where an immaculately made-up girl had shown her how to transform herself into a woman so sophisticated and alluring that she was almost unrecognisable.

It was as well she still had her French cheque-book, Kate thought as she laid the collection of eye-shadows, blushers, foundation and mascara out in front of her. It had been an expensive whim, and it wasn't as if the cosmetics had been her only expense!

She almost lost her nerve when she sat back and looked at the final effect. Her eyes looked huge and sultry, her mouth provocative with its bold outline of red lipstick. The blushers and highlighters had been used more subtly, but no less effectively.

She looked stunning.

She would never be able to carry it off, Kate realised in panic, but it was ten to seven, and there was no time to take it all off and start again. Hurriedly drying her hair, she stepped into the dress she had bought and smoothed it down in front of the mirror.

She had never worn a dress like it. It was black, with short sleeves and a plain round collar that somehow made the slash at the cleavage all the more dramatic. Kate leant forward experimentally and winced. It hadn't seemed quite that revealing in the shop. She would have to sit bolt upright all evening!

Kate studied her reflection with a sense of shock. The dress stopped just above her knees, and the high-heeled shoes merely emphasised the length of her slim legs. She had never looked like this before, with that bright challenging look in her eyes and the wanton provocation of face and figure.

There was a sharp rap on the door and Luke's voice called, 'Ready?' impatiently.

A small smile curved Kate's mouth as her doubts suddenly disappeared. Even if Luke sacked her, he would remember her this time!

She picked up her bag and jacket and opened the door just as Luke raised his hand to knock again.

For a long moment he just stared at her, and then his hand fell slowly to his side.

'I'm ready,' said Kate brightly, stepping past him and pulling the door closed behind her.

Luke's eyes dropped to her legs, and then travelled accusingly upwards to her face. 'I didn't buy you that dress!'

'This old thing? No, I brought it with me. I thought it might come in handy.'

'Did you, indeed?' he said grimly. 'And what about all those clothes I bought you?'

'They're very nice, of course, but I'm allowed to wear some of my own clothes, surely?'

'I'd have preferred it if you'd worn something a little more...suitable. This is a business dinner we're going to, not a nightclub. Perhaps you could remember that?' Luke's face was a mask of disapproval. This was the man who must have seen Helen in far more *risqué* outfits!

Kate was unrepentant. She felt heady with a sense of her own power tonight. 'Don't be so stuffy, Luke. No one could possibly object to a black dress for dinner.'

'It depends on how you wear it! And why are you all made up like that?' Luke asked grumpily as they walked down to the lift. 'I suppose all this effort is for Xavier's benefit? Don't tell him you've fallen for that pseudo-French charm!'

'I'm half-French myself—remember?—and I can assure you that there's nothing pseudo whatsoever about his charm,' Kate said sweetly, knowing it would annoy him. 'You could learn a lot from him!'

The lift doors whispered open and she swept inside, followed by a scowling Luke. The lift was lined with mirrors and their reflections multiplied around them. Kate risked a peek at Luke. He looked dark and dangerous in his formal suit.

He glanced at her and she looked quickly away, tilting her chin unconsciously.

'I must say, this is a new side to you, Kate,' he said. 'I'd never expected you were the kind of girl to own a dress like that.'

'There's a lot you don't know about me.'

'So it seems. How often do you wear it?'

'Oh, quite a lot.'

'Seems funny that you haven't got round to taking off the price tag, in that case,' Luke said sardonically, reaching over to pull the tag out of the neckline behind her.

The nape of her neck shivered where his fingers brushed against it, and colour stained her cheeks as she pulled herself away to tear off the tag resentfully. If he had given her a little more time she would have noticed it herself.

On Xavier's recommendation, she had booked a restaurant in the rue de Buci, a narrow street on the Left Bank. It was already crowded when they arrived, the waiters with their long white aprons threading their way skilfully between the tables.

Kate was in a feisty mood, and kept up a flow of gay conversation while they waited for Philippe and Xavier to arrive, in spite of a distinct lack of encouragement from Luke. When they appeared she greeted them warmly, and was gratified by their admiring attention.

Business was soon disposed of and the discussion became more general. Kate sparkled and flirted outrageously with Xavier while she watched Luke out of the corner of her eyes. He was making a heroic effort to look as if he was enjoying himself, but a muscle worked steadily in his jaw.

Later she could remember little about the meal. She remembered Xavier's caressing eyes resting on her cleavage as she leant forward to pick up her glass, and Philippe's aloof face, warm with amusement. There was a moment of strange lucidity when she caught a glimpse of herself in a mirror, and she remembered thinking that it was like looking at a stranger with flushed cheeks, reckless glittering eyes and over-bright smile. There must be more of her mother in her than she had thought!

She remembered Luke, too. His hands gesturing as he talked to Philippe. The swift smile that didn't include her. The angle of his head as he spoke to the waiter. And once, when she looked up, she found herself staring straight into his implacable slate-hard eyes, unable to look away until he turned away indifferently, leaving her to gulp at her wine and feel suddenly hot.

Xavier, delighted with his vivacious companion, was all for taking Kate on to a nightclub afterwards, but, before she could open her mouth to refuse, a boot-faced Luke was doing it for her.

'Kind of you,' he said curtly, 'but I'm going to need Kate to do some work for me first thing tomorrow morning.'

Xavier looked as if he was about to protest, but Philippe was nodding. 'Yes, we should all go home.' He held out his hand to Luke. 'I have a meeting with my directors tomorrow at nine. Come to my office at eleven and I will let you have a decision then.'

CHAPTER SEVEN

KATE barely had time to say goodnight before Luke had taken her arm and practically dragged her down the street while she was still trying to wave to Xavier.

'The taxi rank's the other way,' she protested.

'We're walking back. I could do with some air, and you certainly need to clear your head.'

'I feel fine,' Kate said bravely.

'You won't tomorrow, and, despite the fact that it's obviously the least of your concerns, you're here to work for me. I shall need you in the morning, and you won't be any use to me with a crashing hangover!'

Buoyed up by wine and admiration, Kate was unrepentant. 'I shan't have one. I haven't had that much to drink.'

'That's what you think! I thought I made it clear earlier on that this was a business dinner?'

'Perfectly clear, thank you.'

'Then why didn't you behave as if it was?' Luke demanded furiously. 'Instead of tarting yourself up like a dog's dinner and leaning all over Xavier so he could get a good look at your cleavage?

Anyone watching you would have known that business was the last thing on your mind!'

'If we have to walk,' Kate interrupted him, 'you'll have to slow down. I can't run in high heels!'

Infuriated by her insouciant attitude, Luke ignored her and strode on. 'That dress is downright indecent!'

'You wouldn't have objected if Helen had been wearing it!'

'Helen is not my secretary,' Luke said icily. 'You are. I think you should remember who pays your very generous salary occasionally!'

'I can hardly forget with you reminding me every five minutes!' Kate snapped. 'And my dress is *not* indecent. It's smart and discreet.'

'What's discreet about a bloody great slit down your cleavage? Xavier could hardly take his eyes off it!'

'It might be a little revealing when I lean forward,' Kate allowed, 'but I didn't do that very often.'

'We all got an eyeful every time you picked up your glass,' Luke said brutally. 'And, since you seemed intent on drinking us all under the table, that was more than often!'

'Oh, rubbish!' Kate said crossly. She shook her arm free and stopped under an ornate street-light. 'Look, can we please sit down? I've got a stitch already.'

Luke circled her in frustration. 'I don't know what's got into you, Kate. You used to be so quiet and businesslike, but since you've been in Paris you've become some kind of *femme fatale*!'

'And whose fault is that?' Kate retorted. 'Who made me cut my hair? Who made me change my clothes? I think you ought to make up your mind what you want, Luke. You insisted I try to look sophisticated. Don't I do that?'

Luke hunched a shoulder. 'Yes.'

'So what's the problem?'

His jaw worked furiously as he glared at her, bent under the street-light, rubbing her calves.

'I don't like it,' he admitted grudgingly at last. 'Every time I see you you've turned into someone different.'

Kate straightened slowly. Luke looked cross and baffled, and quite suddenly all her anger and bravado fell away from her. All at once everything seemed very clear and distinct, as if a fog of swirling emotions had lifted. Luke stood tensely in the pool of light, watching her. He seemed overwhelmingly solid and well-defined against the blurred darkness of the street behind him.

'It's skin-deep,' she assured him gently. 'I might look a bit different, but underneath I'm still the same plain, boring secretary!'

The angry set of his shoulders relaxed. 'You were never plain, Kate, and you were certainly never boring.' He smiled slightly. 'But I hope that you are still the same.'

The strained, angry atmosphere that had smouldered between them since Luke had kissed her had dissolved suddenly, to be replaced by one that was sweeter but infinitely more dangerous.

'Well, I am,' Kate said in a no-nonsense tone as she struggled not to respond to the tug of his smile.

'That sounds more like the Kate we know and——' there was an infinitesimal pause before he completed the cliché '—and love.'

His last word hung in the air between them, and Kate's heart began to thud slowly, painfully, as he looked at her across the pool of light.

She rubbed her arms. 'It's cold,' she said to break the silence. 'Shall we keep moving?'

'We can get a taxi if you'd like. Those shoes do wonders for your legs, but probably not your feet!'

'No, I'd like to walk,' Kate said. 'I'll be all right.'

It was a clear moonlit night, and the air was cool against her cheeks as they walked in silence down to the Seine and across the Pont St-Michel to the Ile de la Cité. They stood on the bridge for a while and watched the lights shimmering on the river.

People passed them silently, as if on the backdrop to a film in which Kate and Luke were the only characters. Kate stared at the awe-inspiring lines of Notre-Dame, illuminated against the night-sky, and was aware only of Luke beside her, not touching her, his profile absorbed.

'I'm sorry if I lost my temper,' Luke said gruffly to the still, oily waters below.

It was so unexpected that Kate caught her breath. 'I'm sorry if I behaved badly,' she apologised to the cathedral in a small voice.

There was a pause. She glanced sideways to find him watching her. It was too dark to see the colour of his eyes, but they gleamed in the reflected light. He smiled at her and, filled with wordless happiness, she smiled back.

'Come on,' he said, taking her arm. 'Let's get back to the hotel.'

They walked slowly past the Louvre and through the back streets. Kate felt as if they were alone in Paris; there was only Luke's hand beneath her arm and his reassuring strength at her side. They didn't talk much, but the silence between them was an easy one.

Once they stopped in front of a *fromagerie* to admire the mouth-watering array of cheeses displayed in the windows. There were huge Roqueforts and creamy Bries, great rubbery-looking chunks of Gruyère and jars of little goats' cheeses stacked in herbed oil, homely cheeses and eye-catching cheeses in every shape and size.

Luke was pointing at a Chèvre, but Kate hardly heard what he said. She was watching his hand, remembering how it had slid to the nape of her neck, warm and strong. Her eyes skittered up to his mouth and she wondered how it would feel if he kissed the sensitive skin just below her earlobe, where her jaw met the long line of her throat. It quivered at the thought, and a wrench of desire twisted her so unexpectedly that she took a quick indrawn breath, dragging her eyes back to the window. She stared blindly ahead, fighting down the desire to lean against the man so close beside her, to slide her hands over his broad chest, to press her lips against the pulse beating in his throat, to pull his head down for her kiss.

'Are you all right, Kate?' Luke looked down at her with concern.

'Yes,' she said in a strangled voice, stepping away from the bright light of the window so that he couldn't see her face clearly, but inwardly she despaired as appalled realisation washed over her.

She was in love with Luke.

As Luke had promised, Kate woke the next morning feeling distinctly seedy. The night before was a blur, interspersed with vivid flashes of memory: the restaurant, Notre-Dame illuminated, the *fromagerie* and the appalled realisation of how hopelessly in love she had fallen.

Or had she been in love with him all along?

Kate splashed cold water on her face and then stared at herself in the bathroom mirror as she patted her skin with a towel. Droplets of water clung to her lashes, and her eyes looked dark and anguished, reflecting the pounding in her head and the ache in her heart.

It had been madness to tangle with Luke again. She should have just walked away. There would have been other jobs. She *knew* what he was like.

He didn't want to be loved the way she loved him. He liked his women cynical and detached. He liked his secretaries cool and collected. And she was his secretary, so, if that was what he wanted, that was what she would be. Luke must never guess how she felt.

When he rapped at her door she jumped. Be businesslike, she chided herself, wrapping her robe more closely around her as if in protection. Let him think you're as brisk and professional as ever.

'You look terrible,' Luke said after one look at her. 'I knew you were going to suffer this morning!'

'I haven't got a hangover,' Kate lied with dignity. 'I just feel a little fragile.'

'Serves you right for wearing a dress like that,' Luke said unsympathetically, but his eyes travelled over her bare face and sleep-tousled hair with some amusement. 'I must say, it makes a change to see you looking less than immaculate!'

He was wearing a grey suit and was clearly ready to start work.

Kate wondered how he managed to look so revoltingly awake and energetic. 'I'm not used to drinking so much wine,' she explained.

'Believe me, nobody would have guessed from your performance last night!' He reached into his inside pocket and produced a packet of aspirin. 'Here, take two of these,' he said gruffly. 'There's no need to rush. I'm going out, but I'll be back later and we'll go to see Robard together.'

By the time he returned Kate was dressed in the same skirt as the day before, but with a thin olive-green jumper, which made her look businesslike, even if she didn't feel the part.

They had to wait in Philippe Robard's office for nearly forty minutes. Luke was on edge and prowled around the room, trying to convince himself that they would get the contract. Kate longed to put her arms round him reassuringly, but his nervousness was catching, and she sat primly on a chair, hoping desperately that she hadn't ruined all his chances by her behaviour last night.

'Where is Robard?' Luke glanced at his watch yet again. 'It can't take them that long to come to a decision.'

'Philippe did tell us that some of the directors are keen on giving the contract to a French firm.'

'I'm offering them a better deal,' Luke countered, as if trying to convince her. 'They have to give it to us. We've got the experience and the expertise.'

'You haven't had experience dealing with Frenchmen, though,' Kate said, playing devil's advocate.

'No, but you have,' Luke said nastily, 'judging by how you dealt with Xavier last night!'

The door opened before Kate had a chance to point out that there was no need for him to take out his nervousness on her, and Philippe Robard came in.

'Please accept my apologies, Monsieur Hardman,' he said, shaking hands with them both. 'I have kept you waiting, but the board has, at last, come to a decision. We will accept your proposal.'

Luke drew a deep breath of relief, and then smiled. 'Thank you,' he said simply.

'I have to admit that there was opposition to using an untried English firm, but Xavier and I were able to persuade them that with the involvement of Mademoiselle Finch there would be no problems of communication.'

Delighted, Kate glanced at Luke, but after that first betraying smile he had his excitement well under control and was calmly agreeing to discuss details of the next stage of the contract at a later date, so she maintained a businesslike front as well while Philippe escorted them courteously downstairs and said goodbye to them on the steps.

Without saying a word, Luke and Kate began to walk sedately away, but, once out of sight of Philippe, Luke stopped.

'He gave us the contract,' he said, as if he had only just realised.

'Yes, he did.' Kate smiled at his expression. 'He must have liked my dress after all!'

At that, Luke swung her into his arms with an exuberant laugh. 'We did it!' he exulted, and Kate laughed delightedly, caught up in the excitement.

They both became aware at the same time how close he was holding her, but Luke didn't release her immediately. Instead he looked down into her bright face, and his own smile faded while a much more disturbing light began to burn in his eyes.

For a long moment they just stared at each other, then Luke's hands tightened against her.

He's going to kiss me, Kate thought in panic, knowing that she would not be able to resist and terrified of how revealing her response would be.

But he didn't kiss her. He released her slowly, almost reluctantly. 'I nearly forgot,' he said.

'What?' asked Kate, horrified at how husky her voice sounded.

'Strictly business. That's how you wanted to keep things, wasn't it?'

He looked at her closely, almost as if he was waiting for her to disagree, but Kate nodded. It was better this way. 'Yes,' she said.

'You said it was more sensible.'

It was. Hard, but sensible. 'Yes,' she said again.

There was a tiny pause. Luke folded the collar of her jacket down and patted it in place. 'We'd better celebrate,' he said after a moment.

He took her to a café in a small cobbled courtyard near the hotel, where they drank a bottle of Sauvignon and ate goat's cheese with a rye bread that was hard and dry and delicious. The momentary awkwardness had passed and they talked easily, planning how the contract would work and what changes would need to be made in the office.

It was too cold to sit outside, so they chose a small round table in the window. Kate moved her glass around on the plastic top, leaving interlocking damp circles until Luke told her not to make such a mess and wiped it up with a paper napkin.

Kate was happy, she realised with a small shock of surprise. Luke was more likely to break her heart than ever return her love, but here in this warm café, with Paris passing by outside and the brusque difficult man absorbed in his work on the other side of the table, she was content.

Resting her crossed arms on the table, she leant forward and gazed out of the window. Two old ladies, identically dressed in black, stood and gossiped on the cobbles. One had a tartan shopping trolley, and a long loaf of French bread stuck out at a jaunty angle. The other seemed to be complaining with much gesticulating and shrugging and grimacing.

Kate's autumn-coloured eyes were soft, and a faint smile lifted the corners of her mouth as she watched the scene.

'What's so funny?' Luke asked.

'I'm just happy,' she said simply.

'Hmmnn.' Luke gave her a look of mock suspicion. 'I never thought any secretary of mine would describe herself as happy. Most of them seemed to spend half their time in tears, complaining that I bullied them,' he remembered morosely.

Laughter danced in her eyes. 'You probably did.'

'I bully you, but you don't cry.'

'Perhaps I should!'

'Please don't. I never had the patience to deal with the watering-pots. As far as I was concerned, if they couldn't put up with a little shouting they shouldn't have been working for me.' He paused and studied Kate's face thoughtfully. 'I've been through no less than twelve secretaries in the last two years alone. You're the only one who's ever stood up to me.'

'Well, you're not so bad,' Kate teased. She felt absurdly happy. Careful, she warned herself. Keep things light. It would be easy to blurt out how much she loved him and spoil everything. At least this way she could be near him during the day. 'I get to sit in a Paris café every now and then. I'm easily pleased.'

Luke hesitated, then reached into his jacket pocket to pull out a small, beautifully wrapped box. 'Since you're so easy to keep happy, I suppose I don't need to give you this, but I'd like you to have it.' He put it on the table in front of her and Kate stared down at it in astonishment. 'I was going to give it to you when we got back to London,' he explained a little awkwardly. 'It's to thank you for helping me to get the contract. I know I wouldn't have been able to do it without you.'

'But Luke...' Kate didn't know what to say. She picked up the little box as if it were very fragile. 'You really didn't need to. I was just doing my job.'

'If you can call your performance last night doing your job...!' Both of them were glad to ease the embarrassment with laughter. 'They wrapped it in the shop,' Luke went on as she pulled at the curled ribbon.

'I rather thought they might have done!' It was impossible to imagine Luke's massive hands managing anything as fiddly as this delicate wrapping.

The paper fell away to reveal a small leather jeweller's box. With a startled look at Luke, Kate opened it carefully. An exquisite brooch lay on a bed of silk. It was rather an old-fashioned design, with simple scrolls of gold on either side of a lustrous pearl.

Kate felt tears sting her eyes. 'It's beautiful,' she said huskily.

'I thought you might use it to pin the cleavage on that black dress together,' Luke said severely, but he was clearly pleased at her reaction. Seeing Kate's mouth tremble, he added, 'You're not going to turn into a watering-pot after all?'

'No.' Kate shook her head so that the shining hair bounced, and sniffed unromantically. Pushing back her chair, she half stood to lean over the table and lay her palm against his face. 'Thank you,' she murmured, and kissed his cheek. His skin was tantalisingly rough, with a clean, indefinably male scent.

Luke's hand came up to cover hers, and tightened over it as she pulled away, so that he was still holding it as she sat down, suddenly shy.

'You never wear any jewellery,' he said, turning her hand over and inspecting her fingers. 'Why is that?'

'I'm afraid I've got expensive tastes,' Kate said a little unsteadily. She was excruciatingly aware of his warm touch. His fingers were strong and dry, slightly rough against the smoothness of hers. 'I'd rather not wear anything until I have something worth wearing—like this brooch.'

'It's a pity. You've got beautiful hands. I noticed them the first time I met you. You never paint your nails, do you? They're just cut short and kept very clean.' He rubbed his thumb over one of her nails experimentally.

Only their fingertips were touching, but Kate could feel desire quivering deep inside her. Her skin tingled and her face grew hot as longing shivered along her veins, clenching her stomach with the steady, insistent tug of physical yearning.

'Perhaps someone will buy you some rings some day,' he went on.

'Perhaps,' she croaked, then cleared her throat hastily.

Luke's eyes were unreadable. 'Make sure he doesn't buy you diamonds. Diamonds are too hard for you. You need warmer stones, rubies or emeralds or pearls. Or topaz, to match your eyes.'

With a supreme effort Kate pulled her hand away. 'It's not an immediate problem,' she said shortly. He wasn't being fair. Didn't he know how her heart soared just to be near him? Couldn't he see how she burned at his touch?

She was his secretary. She must remember that. Cool. Sensible. Businesslike. Wasn't that how she had decided to be? Wasn't that how she was?

Kate closed the lid of the box and turned it slowly between her hands, her head bent so that all Luke could see was the dark sweep of her lashes against the clear skin.

'No, I suppose not,' he said in a flat voice.

The companionable atmosphere had tensed, and the silence that fell jangled uneasily between them. Kate found that she was holding the box too tightly, and put it down, hiding her hands beneath the table in case Luke should see their shaking.

She stared blindly down at the plastic ashtray advertising Gauloises. Luke's face danced in front of her eyes: firm nose, firm mouth, firm jaw. The line of his cheek, the lines around his eyes. She ached with the need to reach out and touch him.

Suddenly Luke picked up his glass and tossed back the dregs of his wine. 'Come on,' he said, putting the glass back down with an abrupt click. 'We'd better go if we want to catch that flight.'

It was a silent journey back to London. Luke buried himself in a report, and Kate looked out of the window at the blue lightness above the clouds and reminded herself of all the reasons why she shouldn't love him.

It was pointless. It was stupid. It was a complete waste of her life. He wasn't even very nice. She would do far better to fall in love with someone who would appreciate her, like Xavier. The sensible thing to do would be to convince herself that Paris had gone to her head. She would concentrate on her work and forget that Luke was anything other than her boss.

Well, she would try.

CHAPTER EIGHT

FORTUNATELY for Kate, so much needed to be done to finalise details for the new contract that she had little time to think, and when she was able to go into work with a calm pulse and a heart that did no more than lift very slightly when Luke came into the room she decided that she had simply been over-reacting to the excitement of Paris.

She and Luke had slipped into a routine of sheer hard work, and Kate often had to work late, translating or collating documents when the phones stopped ringing at the end of the day. She didn't mind. The longer she worked, the less time she had to think about whom Luke was taking out to dinner.

He seemed tired and preoccupied much of the time, but it didn't stop his going out every night, either with Helen or a girl called Lynette, who rang persistently, usually when Kate was at her busiest.

She and Luke had found an even balance, Kate decided. Apart from one or two notable occasions, Luke was generally polite and treated her as a valued and efficient employee. Kate told herself she was glad. Once or twice she would look up from her word processor and their eyes would meet for a glancing moment before both looked quickly away.

One day Luke came into the office, to find Kate holding a huge bunch of roses and searching for the card.

'Who's been sending you flowers?' he scowled.

Kate opened the envelope and pulled out the card. 'They're from Xavier,' she said slowly, reading the message.

'Xavier! What's he doing, sending you flowers?' Luke snatched the card out of her hand. '"Hoping to see you soon, Xavier,"' he read with disgust. 'When's he coming?'

'I've no idea,' said Kate. 'I'm surprised he didn't mention it on the phone. I speak to him quite often.'

'I hope you're not using the office phone to organise your love-life,' Luke said ungraciously. 'I won't have my staff making personal phone calls all day.'

Kate cast him a look of calm reproof. 'You know perfectly well that I have to talk to Xavier about business. He's dealing with most of the detail on the contract. It's one of the reasons you employ me, after all, to talk to him about the arrangements in French.'

'As long as they're the only arrangements you're talking about!' Luke went into his office and shut the door behind him with a bang.

The flowers seemed to put Luke out of temper for the rest of the day. He was in a nit-picking mood and nearly drove Kate up the wall by finding fault with everything she did, and changing his mind about some travel arrangements so often that Kate had difficulty holding on to her temper.

But it was a beautiful February day, and the sky was bright with the promise of spring. Pale winter sunshine poured in through the window and the sweet fragrance of the roses hung in the air. In spite of Luke, Kate found herself humming as she went through some papers on her desk.

'What are you so happy about?' Luke snapped, erupting from his office without warning. He strode over to the filing cabinets and began rummaging around in one of the drawers. 'I suppose you're feeling smug because of those roses cluttering up the office?'

'Are you looking for anything in particular?' Kate asked sweetly, ignoring his question.

'I want that file on David Young Associates. Why can't you keep these files in some kind of order?'

'They are in order. You're looking in the wrong drawer.' Kate rose, pushed him firmly out of the way, shut the drawer and pulled out the one beneath it. 'The David Young Associates file lives here,' she said, retrieving a thick buff folder. 'It's difficult to find, I know, because the label is confusingly marked "David Young Associates".'

Luke glared at her sarcasm and grabbed the file from her as the phone rang.

Kate answered it. 'It's for you,' she said to Luke. 'Helen Slayne. I think it must be a personal call.'

Luke took the receiver with bad grace and a look which said that he had not missed the point. 'Yes, Helen, what is it...? No, I can't be any nicer. I'm busy.' He was obviously regretting taking the call in front of Kate, for he turned away and lowered his voice. 'I'm *not* ignoring you. I've just got a lot on my mind at the moment.'

There was a pause. Kate, studiously carrying on with her paperwork, could imagine Helen's sultry murmurings. Luke watched her suspiciously over his shoulder as he listened. His gaze fell on the roses and he glowered at them. 'All right,' he said. 'Come in later and I'll take you out to lunch.'

He banged down the phone. 'I'm going out to lunch,' he said unnecessarily, still glaring at the flowers.

'That'll be nice.' Kate kept her voice bland. 'Would you like me to book you a table?'

Luke's jaw was working in the way it did when he was trying to control his temper. 'I'll do it myself!' he said rudely, and banged back into his office.

Kate raised her eyes heavenwards. There was no pleasing him today! It would be a relief to have him out of the office for a couple of hours.

She was frowning over some shorthand when Helen made her entrance. She looked breathtaking as usual in leopard-patterned leggings and a provocatively cut top in a dull gold colour. Really, Luke had a nerve criticising her black dress for being revealing, Kate remembered indignantly.

A pair of sunglasses pushed on top of her head held the glorious silver-blonde mane away from Helen's face as she sauntered over to Luke's door with barely a glance at Kate.

When she emerged with Luke a few minutes later Luke was looking grumpy. He stopped to give Kate a number where she could reach him if necessary.

'Don't tell me you've got *another* secretary, darling!' Helen said lightly, deigning to notice Kate's existence at last. 'The other one didn't last long, did she? What *do* you do to them?'

'What other one?' Luke asked irritably, still looking through his diary for the number of the restaurant.

'The last time I came round there was a rather plain, disapproving-looking female sitting here.'

'Kate was here then. Nobody could be more disapproving than her!'

'Really?' Helen's green eyes sharpened as she took in the fact that Kate was not nearly as plain as she remembered. 'Quite a transformation!' She didn't sound as if she liked the fact.

Kate's lips tightened as Helen looked at her a little more closely.

'You know, there's something familiar about you,' Helen said slowly.

Luke had finished scribbling the number down and now tucked his diary back in his inside pocket. 'Funny, I keep thinking that, too.'

Kate tensed as they both stared at her with narrowed eyes.

'Must be someone on television,' Luke said, giving up.

'Perhaps you're right.' Helen sounded unconvinced. 'I wouldn't have said that we move in the same social circles, that's for sure!'

Kate's eyes were cold. 'I expect I look familiar because you've seen me before,' she said briskly, hoping that her dismissive tone would divert Helen's attention from the real truth of what she said. 'Luke was right. I was sitting here last time you came round.'

'That must be it.' Helen shrugged, losing interest as Luke took her arm.

'Let's get a move on,' he said impatiently.

Kate watched them go to the door before allowing herself to relax with a sigh of relief. Unfortunately, Helen chose that moment to glance back over her shoulder, and her eyes narrowed suspiciously at the relief writ large in Kate's expression.

Kate could only hope that she and Luke would have better things to talk about than how familiar his secretary looked. If they thought about it long enough they might remember, and that was the last thing she wanted!

She was waiting nervously when Luke came back after lunch. He didn't say anything, so she breathed again, but he was in a foul mood and kept her working until half-past six.

Kate arrived punctually at nine the following morning, to find Luke prowling around her office and muttering as he rifled through files. Evidently his temper hadn't improved overnight!

Kate judged it best simply to ignore him. She wished him a cool good morning, which was not acknowledged, and hung up her coat. When he was in this kind of mood she had no trouble telling herself that she must have imagined falling in love with him!

The phone rang as she headed towards her desk, and, although she had plenty of time to answer it, Luke jumped on it as if to prove that she wasn't doing her job properly.

'Yes?' he snapped, obviously about to take his bad temper out on some poor unsuspecting employee at the other end of the line, but he was to be frustrated. With some amusement, Kate heard him say, with an effort to sound polite, 'Oh, yes, how are you?'

Obviously a client, Kate thought, seating herself behind her desk and reaching for the diary. He wasn't polite to anyone else.

There was a pause and then Luke said stiffly, 'Yes, she's here.' He handed the receiver to Kate. 'It's Xavier Robard, wanting to speak to my *charming assistant*,' he said nastily. 'I presume that means you.'

Kate took the phone from him with a brilliant smile and proceeded to greet Xavier with a lot more warmth than she did normally. Luke gave her no chance to be private, but remained obstinately perched on her desk, pretending to read a file but patently eavesdropping. Kate was speaking in rapid French, but she had no doubt that he was following the gist of the conversation.

'So when's he coming over?' Luke demanded as she put down the phone.

'Oh, did you miss that bit?' Kate asked sarcastically. 'Sorry, I should have spoken more slowly for you!'

Their eyes clashed angrily. His were slate-grey and very hard, hers a hostile gold.

'He's coming tomorrow,' Kate added sulkily, looking away first.

'And you're having dinner with him.' It was a statement, not a question.

'Yes. Do you have any objection?'

Luke grunted for an answer. 'Is he coming into the office?'

'He didn't say so. Why, did you want to see him particularly?'

'You might have thought that I might have some details to discuss with him!' Luke said unreasonably.

'I can easily ring him and make an appointment if that's the case.' Kate reached for the phone, but Luke stopped her with an irritable gesture.

'Oh, leave it! If he's coming panting after you he probably won't want to be bothered about business.'

'As a matter of fact, he's coming over on a quite different business matter,' Kate said coldly.

Luke snorted. 'That's his story!' He picked up the desk calendar. 'Tomorrow's the fourteenth—Valentine's Day. Funny that his *different business* should just happen to be tomorrow. I suppose he chose the date deliberately?'

'I think that's most unlikely,' Kate said with a frosty look. 'They don't make a big thing of Valentine's Day in France.'

'Well, since you've reminded me of it, I suppose I'd better arrange for some flowers for Helen and Lynette,' Luke said with what Kate strongly suspected was deliberate provocation. 'Get a bouquet sent to each of them tomorrow, will you?'

'What, both of them?'

'Why not?' he retorted cynically. 'It'll keep them both quiet, and they don't need to know that they're not the only ones.'

Kate made a neat note on her shorthand pad. She was determined not to be upset by the fact that Luke chose to send flowers to other girls. 'What sort of bouquet?' she asked, very matter-of-fact.

'Oh, I don't know.' Luke shrugged irritably. 'One of those big elaborate jobs. Whatever you would like.'

'Personally, I think those big bouquets are rather vulgar,' Kate said austerely. 'A simple bunch of tulips, hand-delivered, would be much more romantic.'

'You're so understated, Kate!' Luke got to his feet, a hint of amusement in his voice. 'Still, I think vulgar bouquets would be much more appropriate for Helen and Lynette.' He glanced down at the flowers Xavier had sent and his expression hardened once more. 'Send them a dozen red roses each.'

'Any message?' Kate asked sweetly. 'Or would you like me to make one up for you?'

'Just put my name on them,' Luke said with a nasty look.

'Very romantic,' Kate murmured as he turned away.

'I'm not a romantic,' he snarled, heading for his office. 'And nor are Helen or Lynette.'

'Then why bother sending them flowers?'

'It gives them some kind of trophy to display, that's all. And, if all it takes is money, I don't care!'

No, Luke was definitely not a good man to fall in love with.

Kate phoned the florist and tried not to think about Valentine's Day. A day for lovers. It wasn't a good day to be hopelessly in love with someone who didn't, would never, love you.

She woke the next morning feeling unusually depressed, and she went through her routine of getting ready without enthusiasm. When the doorbell rang she struggled into her dressing-gown and opened the door, expecting to see the postman with something that was too big to fit through the letter-box. Probably a bill, she thought glumly. He certainly wasn't likely to have a pile of Valentine's cards for her!

There was no one there. Kate looked out, puzzled, and then her gaze dropped to the doorstep. A large bunch of pink tulips, still tightly bundled, lay there.

Kate picked them up slowly. There was no message.

What was it she had said? *A simple bunch of tulips would be much more romantic.* Closing the door behind her, she buried her face in the flowers with a slow smile. They could only be from Luke. Her heart soared even as her mind struggled to keep it firmly under control.

'I'm not a romantic'—but he had given her flowers. Of course, it might be a gesture from a busy man to say that her hard work did not go as unnoticed as she thought. Yes, it might be that. Kate put the tulips in a glass jug and stood back to admire them. It would be just like Luke to do something confusing like this rather than just come out with a compliment!

She speculated about the flowers all the way to work, unable to decide whether she should thank him, or whether he would prefer her to pretend she didn't know whom they were from.

In the event, he solved her dilemma by being out of the office all morning, and in such a bad mood when he finally came in that Kate decided to restrict her comments to the bare necessities. When he had snapped her head off for the fourth time she even began to wonder if she had been mistaken, and was thankful that she hadn't said anything.

'I suppose you want to leave early, since you're going out with your Frenchman tonight?' Luke grumbled as she laid some letters on his desk.

'I don't need to leave early, but I'd certainly like to leave on time for once.' Kate looked back at him calmly.

'There's no need to sound such a martyr. Anyone would think I kept you chained to this desk twenty-four hours a day!'

'I don't usually get away before half-past six,' Kate pointed out, unruffled.

Luke chewed at his thumbnail. 'Where's he taking you?'

'I'm not sure—it's a restaurant he knows in Soho somewhere.'

'Xavier *would* know a little restaurant in Soho!' Luke snorted with disgust and then glared at her suspiciously. 'What are you going to wear? Not that black dress, I hope?'

'I'm afraid I haven't given it much thought yet,' Kate said frostily, resenting the inquisition. What did it matter to him? He had already asked her to book a table for dinner that night, so he obviously had plans of his own.

Kate had grown more and more crabby as the day had passed, and she began to feel foolish about her euphoria over the flowers. Even if he had sent them, it hadn't been the romantic gesture she had hoped. He was far too busy having a good time with Helen or Lynette or any of the other women who rang up and wasted her time insisting on leaving messages for him.

'Is he going to pick you up from home?' Luke persisted.

Kate sighed, exasperated. She felt like telling him to mind his own business, but that would only stir his curiosity even more. 'I'll probably meet him in town,' she said in a resigned tone. 'He doesn't have a car here, and it would be difficult for him to get to my flat. It's not exactly central.'

'It's not that far,' Luke said, and then stopped as if suddenly realising that he had betrayed himself.

'I didn't realise that you knew where I lived.' Kate lifted one eyebrow coolly, but a treacherous glow of hope began to spread through her.

'Your address is on your CV,' Luke blustered, then grinned a little shamefacedly.

Kate's chill hauteur was no proof against his smile, and even as she warned herself not to give in too easily, she was unable to prevent smiling back.

'Thank you for the flowers,' she said. 'They're lovely.'

'They didn't look much to me.' Luke shuffled the papers on his desk gruffly. 'Can't see why anyone would prefer something like that to a proper bouquet.'

Kate wondered if he was waiting for her to re-assure him that she hadn't read too much into the fact that he had given her flowers.

'There must be something wrong with my taste,' she said lightly. 'How did the roses go down?'

'Received with shrieks of delight, I gather,' Luke said callously, and then looked up at her. She was wearing a straight rust-coloured skirt with the olive-green jumper she had worn in Paris, and looked quietly businesslike. 'I don't suppose you shrieked?'

'No, but I'm sure I liked my tulips more.'

'Really?'

Their eyes met over the desk.

'Really,' she assured him.

'Kate——' Luke began, pushing back his chair, but just then the phone rang. With an exclamation of impatience he snatched up the receiver, and Kate took the opportunity to slip out of the room. She had heard enough to know that it was Helen.

Luke's abrupt swings of mood confused her. One moment he was brusque and cynical, and the next he would look into her eyes and she could swear that the smile that lurked there was for her alone.

Don't do this, Kate, she warned herself. Don't fall in love with him all over again, just when you were doing so well just being his secretary. She sat on the bus, reciting a litany of Luke's faults to herself, as if it were a charm to keep herself immune to his dangerous attraction. If only he would just stick to being rude and unpleasant, it would be so much easier.

She tried to concentrate on the evening ahead, but the first things she saw as she let herself into her flat were the tulips, already starting to open. She loved their clean lines and the graceful droop of their heads, and touched them gently as she went past. They were much nicer than roses.

For Xavier's sake, Kate exerted herself to make an effort. She looked at the black dress hanging in the wardrobe, but in the end chose the jade. The black dress belonged to Luke and that unforgettable walk through the dark, quiet streets of Paris.

Xavier was delighted to see her and full of Gallic charm. Kate found him pleasant and entertaining, but her mind kept drifting off to Luke. She wondered where he was, who he was with, what he was doing. She missed his abrasive presence with a nagging little ache.

This is stupid, she told herself as she smiled and pretended to listen to Xavier. How can you possibly be missing him? You saw him a couple of hours ago, and you'll see more than enough of him tomorrow. He'd only sit there and shout at you.

But still she couldn't wait for the evening to be over.

'And how is Luke?' Xavier was asking.

Impossible. Irresistible. 'He's fine,' said Kate.

'He didn't sound very pleased when I told him I hoped to take you out to dinner. In fact, I wondered if he might have been a bit jealous, *hein*?'

Faint colour tinged Kate's cheekbones. 'Oh, no. He's just funny about mixing business with pleasure.'

'Even though he must do it all the time working with you?' Xavier asked with heavy gallantry. 'He is a hard man!'

Kate ran a finger around the rim of her glass. 'He's just . . . Luke.'

His image rose in front of her as she stared down into her wine: the cold slate eyes that could warm with sudden laughter, the hard mouth that could soften with devastating charm, the strong hands whose merest touch could send her heart into overdrive.

'And you're in love with him,' Xavier said flatly.

Kate looked up. She could deny it, the way she had been trying so hard to deny it to herself, but it was useless. She might as well accept it, and learn to live with it.

'Yes,' she said.

CHAPTER NINE

'WELL,' said Luke, leaning back in his chair after he had finished dictating some letters the next morning, 'how did you get on with Xavier last night?'

'We had a very nice evening, thank you.' Kate ignored the sarcastic edge to his voice as she picked up her notebook and got to her feet. She had no intention of telling Luke that she had spent the whole time thinking about him.

'Very nice? Is that all you can say?' Luke sneered. 'It must have been dull!'

'It wasn't dull. It was...very pleasant.'

'Pleasant!' Luke gave a shout of laughter. 'That's even worse.' He leant over the desk towards her. 'If I'd taken you out on Valentine's Day I'd have made sure that you had an evening that was wild, exciting, unforgettable...anything other than pleasant!'

Kate clutched her notebook defensively in front of her and kept her composure with an effort. 'I might not have enjoyed that so much.'

'Why not? Too daring for you? I can't believe that after the way you were carrying on in Paris!'

The mockery in his voice hurt her. So he had had a wild evening with Helen, had he? He obviously thought she was no fun compared to her.

'Surely it's who you're with on Valentine's Day that matters more than what you do?' she said coldly. 'You don't have to paint the town red to have an unforgettable evening if you're with the right person.'

Luke's face closed. 'How right you are!' he said, and spun round in his chair, effectively dismissing her.

He was withdrawn for the rest of the day. Kate knew that she should have been pleased at having been able to hide her feelings so successfully, but she was restless and miserable, and eagerly accepted Serena's invitation to go and see the latest release at the cinema that evening. The film had been slated in the reviews: mindless entertainment was just what she needed.

It didn't take Serena long to worm the truth out of her. In spite of all Kate's attempts to appear bright and cheerful, her friend brushed aside assurances that she was fine and demanded to know what the matter was. In the end, Kate gave in.

'It's Luke,' she admitted as they queued to buy their tickets.

'I knew it!' Serena crowed. 'You've fallen for him, haven't you?'

Kate nodded, shamefaced.

'It was inevitable,' Serena reassured her. 'I guessed as soon as you started going on about how difficult he was; it was a dead giveaway. I don't blame you. He's terribly attractive, even if he is as awful as you always say he is.'

'He's not awful!' Kate sprang instinctively to Luke's defence, and then subsided. 'Well, not all the time, anyway.'

Serena glanced at her mischievously. 'I thought you said he was rude and arrogant and horrible and thoroughly unpleasant?' she said in an innocent voice, recalling all Kate's phone conversations over the past weeks. 'Not to mention overbearing and unreasonable!'

'He is, but...' Kate trailed off, unable to explain, and Serena rolled her eyes.

'Oh, Kate, you have got it bad!'

'Yes,' Kate said a little wearily. 'I have.'

Serena touched her arm with quick sympathy. 'What does he feel about you?'

'I don't know.' Kate thrust her hands in her pockets and stared glumly down at the pavement. 'Sometimes I think he finds me quite attractive, but the next moment he's being unpleasant again. He wouldn't go out with Helen and Lynette if he was interested in me, would he?'

'He might if he was trying not to be,' Serena said not very clearly. 'He's awfully proprietorial as far as you're concerned, isn't he? Look at the fuss he made about your going out with Xavier! It sounds to me as if he was jealous.'

'You wouldn't have thought so if you'd seen him this morning. He was impossible!' Kate remembered morosely. 'I made the mistake of telling him I'd had a pleasant evening, and he sneered all day, comparing it to the wild, exciting time he'd had with Helen.'

'In that case, he's *definitely* jealous!' Serena said wisely. 'Why don't you tell him how you feel?'

'No!' Kate recoiled instinctively. 'I couldn't possibly.'

'Why not?'

'He doesn't want to get involved with anyone. He's told me as much. He'd hate a clinging, emotional woman.'

'You wouldn't be clinging, though,' Serena pointed out. 'You're not the type.'

'No, but I couldn't be detached either.' Kate's eyes were clear as she turned to look at her friend. 'I love him, Serena. I've never felt like this about anybody before. If it were just a crush I might be able to laugh it off. We might even be able to have a brief affair. That's all he'd be interested in, but that kind of casual physical relationship wouldn't be enough for me.'

She paused. The queue was moving closer to the doors and her eyes fell on a still advertising the film. The hero and heroine were exchanging a passionate embrace. It reminded her of the time Luke had kissed her on the street corner. 'I love all of him,' she went on slowly. 'I love the difficult, annoying things about him as much as the way he looks, or the way he makes me feel. If I can't have all of him I'd rather keep my feelings to myself and carry on as his secretary. That way, neither of us is embarrassed.'

Easy to say, but as the days passed Kate found it more and more difficult to hide her feelings for Luke beneath her aura of cool efficiency. She watched him with a heightened awareness, and flinched whenever he brushed against her inadvertently, reaching for a file or leaning next to her to look at the diary.

She was terrified that he had guessed. The astringent quality in their relationship that had stimulated as well as infuriated her had gradually evaporated. Instead of their snippy exchanges, there were long, awkward silences interspersed with sticky lumps of conversation. They only talked about business and avoided looking at each other.

Kate felt strangely lonely. Luke was remote, detached, and she missed arguing with him more than she would have believed. She even missed his being rude.

Was he trying to warn her off?

She was dreading their return to Paris. The contract was due to be signed the following Tuesday, early in the morning, and Luke had suggested that they fly out the night before to make sure they were there in time. He had even asked if that was agreeable to her! Kate agreed in a colourless tone. Paris held too many memories. She didn't want to go there with this stranger.

The week seemed endless; Kate couldn't decide whether she longed for the weekend, or dreaded it for bringing the Paris trip nearer. She was glad that Solange was coming out of school for the weekend, and planned a non-stop whirl of activities, as much to distract herself as amuse her niece. By the time she had taken Solange back to school on Sunday evening, she was exhausted, but had recovered her composure.

It seemed unbearably intimate to be travelling to the airport together after a largely silent day at the office. Kate stared out of the window of the limousine as it crawled through the rush-hour traffic on the M4 heading towards Heathrow.

If things didn't get any better she would have to start looking for another job. Her heart cracked at the thought of leaving Luke, but he seemed to have put her at a deliberate distance, as if trying to discourage her from getting involved. Kate was humiliated by the idea that her emotions were that transparent. She had been trying so hard to appear unaffected by his sudden change of attitude.

It was after seven by the time they reached the hotel.

'I suppose you've arranged to see Xavier tonight?' Luke said in a distant voice as he signed the register.

'Xavier?' Kate repeated blankly. She had been watching his broad wrist where it emerged from an immaculately white cuff and for a moment couldn't remember quite who Xavier was. 'No.'

Luke glanced at her. Was it her imagination, or did his expression lighten slightly?

'We'd better go and have something to eat together, then,' he said, but in such a colourless voice that she decided that she must have been mistaken.

'All right,' she said, equally wooden.

'Shall we meet down here in half an hour?'

'Fine.'

This is awful, she thought as she washed her face and combed her hair drearily. Everything was so different to the last time they had been here. Even when they had been arguing she had felt excited, *alive*.

Her eye fell on the black dress in her open
suitcase. She had been so angry with Luke when
she had put it on last time! There had been little
point in bringing it, but somehow she had been
reluctant to leave it behind.

Now she picked it up thoughtfully. It was a
wonderful dress, the kind of dress that made you
feel a million dollars. On an impulse, Kate
stripped off her sensible travelling clothes and
slipped it on. If ever she had needed some extra
confidence it was now!

She kept her make-up understated, but at the
last minute pinned the brooch Luke had given
her across the revealing slit. She didn't feel as
exhilarated as the last time she had worn this
dress, but she certainly felt a lot better!

With renewed confidence in her ability to keep
her true feelings hidden from Luke and return to
the relationship they had had before her emotions had started to behave in such a stupid way,
Kate made her way down to the foyer.

Luke was waiting for her. In his grey suit, he
looked taciturn and remote. Hesitating outside
the lift, Kate felt herself stung by unfamiliar pro-
tectiveness as she caught sight of his dark head.
If only he weren't so determined not to depend
on anyone else!

As if aware of her gaze upon him, Luke turned.
Something blazed in his eyes as he saw that she

was wearing the black dress, but the shuttered look dropped back into place almost immediately.

Kate's chin went up at that unmistakable sign of uninterest, and she walked unhurriedly towards him.

'I haven't booked anywhere,' Luke said abruptly as she came up to him. 'I thought we could just walk out and see what we find. I could do with stretching my legs anyway.'

Kate agreed in a neutral voice, and made sure there was a good two feet between them as they walked down the hotel steps and on to the street. Being too close to him would be too much of a temptation.

Lights flashed and blurred as they walked past neon advertisements and garish café signs and impatient cars held up at traffic lights. Horns tooted and pedestrians hurried past; she and Luke seemed to be the only people in Paris not anxious to get to their destination, Kate thought.

They looked at everything except each other until, as they came up to the Place de l'Opéra, Luke suddenly stopped at a crossing, pulling Kate back as she made to step off the kerb.

'Kate, why are you being like this?' he demanded.

Kate looked down at his hand on her sleeve and then up into his face.

'Like what?'

As if aware that he was still holding her, Luke dropped his hands and thrust them into his pockets. 'You've been so distant lately,' he grumbled.

'*I've* been distant?' Kate stared at him in astonishment. 'You're the one who's been distant!'

'No, I haven't!'

'You made it very clear that you were only concerned with work,' she said. 'You discourage every attempt at conversation. Every time I say good morning I feel as if I'm invading your privacy!'

'But that's exactly what I thought about you!' Luke protested. 'After you went out with Xavier you seemed to retreat behind a sort of chilly façade. It was like working with an ice-cube!' He looked down at his shoes. 'I know we used to fight, but after the last time we were here I thought we'd become friends.'

They were blocking the crossing. The crowds pushed past them with fulminating glances and the occasional muttered exclamation, but Luke and Kate were oblivious.

'We were friends,' Kate said.

'Then why aren't we any more? Why did you clam up like that?'

'I thought that was what you wanted. I thought you wanted to keep things strictly business.'

'A businesslike relationship doesn't preclude friendship, does it?' Luke said crossly.

No, but it made it very difficult to be in love at the same time. 'No,' Kate said.

'So you mean all this time I thought you were ignoring me you thought I was ignoring you?'

'Well . . . yes.'

A dangerous smile lurked about his mouth. 'That wasn't very sensible of you, Kate!'

'Whereas you behaved impeccably, I suppose?' Kate retorted, and he laughed, a sudden, exuberant laugh of relief. Despite herself, Kate felt her own mouth quiver in response.

'I've missed the way you answer back when you're cross,' Luke said, holding out his hand. 'Come on, let's shake on a friendly, businesslike relationship with no more misunderstandings, shall we?'

It was what she had wanted, wasn't it? Kate felt his hand close round hers and tried to ignore the jolting response of her heart to his touch, and the small, insistent voice that said that *friendly* and *businesslike* would never be enough.

'Now that that's sorted out, where were we?' Luke asked cheerfully as they crossed the road at last. The grim look he had worn for so long now had vanished and he looked buoyant, even happy.

Kate struggled to match his mood. 'Looking for somewhere to eat.'

'Well, what about here?' They peered at the menu displayed outside a small restaurant. 'We don't need anything grand.'

Inside the restaurant was dark and noisy. It seemed to be full of people talking and laughing and waving their hands about. Kate felt horribly overdressed in her sophisticated black dress, but nobody seemed to notice.

She and Luke were squeezed into a corner, side by side on a plastic *banquette*. Their thighs kept touching, their arms brushing against each other. Luke made no effort to put some space, however small, between them.

Kate's appetite had deserted her. She picked at the trout she had ordered with a creamy herb sauce, and sipped her wine nervously. A candle flickered on the table and she kept her eyes fixed on it, hoping that Luke wouldn't see the desire written on her face.

It was all very well to talk about a friendly relationship, but when Luke's body was pressed so close to hers it was impossible to think about anything but how muscular his thigh felt, how strong his arm. She could see his hands out of the corner of her eye as he lifted his glass or reached for the bread, and wondered how they would feel against her bare skin.

She talked feverishly, unnerved by his eyes on her face, the pressure of his leg against hers, and when at last they stood up to go her knees felt weak. Luke helped her out from behind the table and kept his hand under her arm as they went outside. Kate wanted to pull herself away, but was afraid she would fall.

Luke fell silent as they walked. She had no idea where they were going, but talked on until her tongue felt thick and unwieldy and she floundered to a halt. Instead she looked up at the sky, a narrow strip between the tall Parisian buildings. The moon was almost full, and fuzzy through the reflected city lights.

Kate was ensnared in lassoes of desire, shimmering over her head, shivering down her skin and tightening, tightening, until all she could think about was Luke's mouth, Luke's hands, the feel of his hard body.

Eventually they found themselves back at the hotel. They took the lift to the third floor without touching, without speaking, and walked down the thickly carpeted corridor that muffled even their footsteps. Kate was sure that Luke must hear her heart pounding in the enveloping quiet.

Her hand shook slightly as she unlocked her door and turned to say goodnight.

Luke didn't reply. He just looked at her and then reached out to draw her slowly towards him.

'I don't think this is a very good idea,' Kate managed to whisper, even though she didn't seem to be able to drag her eyes away from his.

'Why not?'

'We... we agreed to keep things strictly business.'

A half-smile lifted the corner of his mouth. 'To hell with business!' he said, and jerked her into his arms.

His kiss was hard and passionate, and Kate was powerless to resist. It was what she had been thinking about all evening, his lips demanding, irresistible, evoking a deep, trembling fire that, once lit, burned quickly out of control.

Kate's arms crept up his arms, around his neck, as her lips sought his in reply. There was a breathless hunger between them, their kisses almost angry as they were swept along on a tide of desire that had been suppressed too long and now threatened to engulf them.

Luke was breathing heavily as he lifted his head and half pushed, half pulled Kate into the room. She collapsed weakly back against the door as he closed it and leant his hands on either side of her.

'I've wanted to kiss you for weeks,' he said, and the husky note in his voice seemed to vibrate through her. 'Every time you came into my office and sat down primly with your notebook and

looked at me with that cool look you have I'd
think about kissing you.' His lips nibbled tantalisingly at the corner of her mouth until Kate
turned her head to meet them with her own. 'I'd
think about kissing you like this,' he murmured
against her parted lips, and pressed her back
against the door.

His hands cupped her face, his fingers tangling
in her hair as their kisses deepened hungrily.

For Kate—sensible, practical, capable Kate—
the past was forgotten and the future abandoned. Nothing mattered but the here and now.
She couldn't have stopped even if she had wanted
to. Her blood was pounding in wild surges of excitement, her body tingling with the instinctive
thrill of response.

Her arms slid beneath his jacket, and she
spread her hands over the smooth cotton of his
shirt. His back was broad and solid and she could
feel his muscles ripple at her touch.

'Did you ever think about kissing me too?'
Luke was demanding, mumbling provocative
kisses along her jaw.

Kate quivered as he reached her ear, the very
spot she had fantasised about as she had stood
in front of the *fromagerie*. 'No,' she gasped,
tipping her head back with luxuriant pleasure.

'You're lying.' She could feel him smile against
her throat. 'Tell me you're lying. Tell me you

wanted me to kiss you.' His hands tightened as he raised his head to look down into her eyes.

'I'm lying. Of course I'm lying,' Kate said with a slow smile as he bent to kiss her again. Her hands were busy pulling out his shirt so that she could slide her hands up and down his skin, warm and smooth and unyielding beneath her fingers.

'Kate!' Luke's breath was ragged as he pulled away slightly. His gaze dropped to the brooch, and he unfastened it with unsteady hands, laying it carefully to one side before turning back and pressing his lips to the shadowy cleft revealed between her breasts.

Arching her head back, Kate felt as if he were plucking at taut strings inside her that stretched and twanged with desire at his very touch. As his lips travelled slowly along her neckline, lingering on the sensitive hollows of her clavicle and the wild pulse in her throat, she pushed the jacket impatiently off his shoulders and fumbled with his tie and the buttons of his shirt.

Her hands were at his belt before he turned her round and undid her zip with agonising slowness, burning kisses down her spine as he went until her skin quivered uncontrollably. There was a rustle as the dress slipped off her shoulders and slithered to the floor.

Kate stepped out of it as if in a dream. The curtains had not yet been drawn and, though the room was in darkness, the moonlight through the window caught her eyes, gleaming with desire.

Her head dropped back as Luke pressed his face into the fragrance of her neck, and her hair brushed softly against him. He turned her back to face him and slid off her underwear to the accompaniment of long, hot kisses.

By the time Luke had discarded his own clothes and pulled her down on to the bed, Kate was on fire. It was heaven to be able to touch him like this, to forget everything in intoxicating abandon, knowing that there could be no stopping now. Their bodies tangled together with increasing urgency and she gasped his name as he ran his hands in insistent exploration over her skin, murmuring endearments against her warmth. His mouth followed the path scorched by his fingers, discovering anew the secret places that reduced Kate to arching, shuddering delight.

Rolling on top of him, she held his face between her hands and smiled down at him before lowering her head very slowly to explore his lips with her own. She lay over him, exulting at the feel of his hardness, of the sensuous thrill of skin against skin.

Luke's arms came up to tighten around her, but she slid downwards, teasing soft, tantalising kisses as she went, until with a groan he rolled her beneath him once more and thrust deep inside her, deeper and deeper until they both cried out in an explosion of release, a shattering of exquisite torment that left them trembling in each other's arms.

Afterwards he held her close. There was no sign of the brusque, arrogant Luke in the man whose warm hands gentled lovingly over her skin.

'Do you still think it wasn't a good idea?' he murmured, kissing the lobe of her ear.

Kate's eyes were closed, but a smile curved her mouth. 'Perhaps it wasn't very sensible.'

'Who wants to be sensible?'

'You did.'

'I've changed my mind. I changed my mind as soon as Xavier took one look at you and saw the same warm, exciting woman as I did under that cool, sensible mask of yours. I could cheerfully have throttled him that night at the restaurant when you were flirting with him. And then, when he took you out and you seemed so different afterwards, I was nearly insane with jealousy.' Luke smoothed the hair away from Kate's flushed face. 'I always thought of you as mine, even when I was pretending you were just another secretary.'

'But I am just a secretary,' she teased, but let her hand drift over his stomach in a gesture that was far from secretarial.

Luke shook his head. 'You're different, Kate. You're the only completely honest woman I've

ever met. How could I resist those clear eyes?'
He kissed her closed lids and, although Kate
smiled, her eyes when she opened them were
troubled.

She *hadn't* been completely honest with him.
Her hands slid around his back to hold him close
while she hesitated. She knew that she ought to
remind him about their brief encounter in the
past, but he was so warm, so close. She didn't
want anything to spoil this moment.

No, she really should tell him... 'Luke,' she
said hesitatingly.

'What is it?' Luke asked, nuzzling kisses
against her throat. His eyes when he lifted his
head to look down into her face were alight with
a warmth that she had never seen there before,
and, despite herself, Kate felt her resolution
crumble. She didn't think she could bear to see
that expression fade, not here, not now. She
would tell him later.

'Oh... nothing.'

Luke's smile almost took her breath away. Who
would have thought that the cold, hard man who
had kissed her all those years ago would have
been capable of such tenderness? 'In that case,
kiss me again!'

'Please?' she reminded him with mock severity.

'Darling Kate, would you mind terribly kissing
me again, please?'

Kate sighed as she pulled him closer. 'If you insist,' she murmured against his mouth, and pushed aside her doubts as she surrendered herself to all-eclipsing joy of the night.

CHAPTER TEN

LUKE woke Kate with kisses early the next morning, but, though his eyes kindled at her stretch of sleepy, luxurious contentment, he wouldn't allow her to linger.

'Wake up!' he said, pulling back the duvet and grinning at her protests. 'We've got a contract to sign, and we're going to be late if we don't hurry!'

He showed Kate his watch and she sat up in horror, all traces of sleep gone as she realised the time. There was no time for breakfast as they dressed quickly and raced across to Philippe Robard's office, but Kate glowed with an inner happiness that no amount of cosmetics and careful dressing could achieve.

Xavier took one look at her and smiled ruefully. 'Luke is a very lucky man,' he said quietly, lifting her hand to his lips in an old-fashioned gesture.

Luke treated her with scrupulous professionalism during the signing, and if Kate had not caught his eye once and seen the light there she might have wondered if this was the same man who had made love to her with such passion last night. But when the contract was signed and they had left the offices he pulled her into his arms in the middle of the street and kissed her as if he had been away for a month.

She had never seen him so elated. Paris was trembling on the edge of spring, and the sun was shining. Kate felt happiness bubbling along her veins like champagne. Everything seemed to have acquired a sharp new focus overnight.

They sat in a café and had a late breakfast, warm buttery croissants and great cups of coffee with steam curling languidly into the sunshine pouring through the windows. Kate rested her elbows, cupping her hands around her cup, and smiled at Luke.

It was wonderful to be able to watch him without restraint, to let her eyes rest on the strong, decisive lines of his face and remember how his skin had felt to her touch last night.

'Don't look like that, Kate,' he grinned, reading her expression easily. 'Or, at least, not when we're in public! I might forget that we have work to do today!'

'You're right.' Kate assumed a demure look. 'We wouldn't want to forget that friendly business relationship we agreed to have, would we?'

Luke reached out and touched her hair gently. 'Not during the day, no, but nights are a different matter! We can forget business then.'

There had been no mention of love, but, as they sat in the sun on that spring morning in Paris, it was enough for Kate.

It was surprisingly easy to slip back into the businesslike role and they worked comfortably together on the plane back to London.

'I'd better go and have a word with Miles,' Luke said when they got back to the office. 'As finance director, he'll need to know the final details we agreed today.'

Kate nodded. She was looking quickly through the day's post, and it was only when the silence lengthened that she looked up in some surprise to see Luke watching her with amusement.

'You look so absorbed,' he said. 'I don't know that I like the way you seem to be able to concentrate on work after what happened last night! Don't say you've forgotten already?'

Kate dropped the letters on to the desk and her clear gaze met his. 'I'll never forget,' she said quietly. 'You know I won't.'

Luke took her hands and pulled her towards him. 'We shouldn't do this,' he muttered.

'*I'm* not doing anything,' Kate pointed out, but she didn't resist as he kissed her.

'You're standing there, looking the way you do. That's enough.'

'This is very unprofessional.' Kate tried to sound severe, but spoiled the effect by sliding her arms round his neck and kissing him back.

'It is. It is.' Luke disentangled himself reluctantly. 'From tomorrow, it's strictly business in the office!'

'Strictly,' Kate agreed with a smile.

'Now I really am going to see Miles.' Luke laid his hand against her cheek for a brief moment. 'Then we'll get down to some work, and then we'll go home—together!'

Kate was still standing by her desk, holding a hand to her cheek where he had touched her, when the door opened suddenly.

She had forgotten Helen.

At the sight of her eclipsing beauty, a cold finger of fear touched Kate's heart and clouded her happiness. What chance did she stand next to Helen? No matter how good she looked, she would always look dim and drab next to the glamorous blonde.

Kate pulled herself together. 'I'm afraid Luke's not here,' she said courteously. 'He's just gone down to have a word with the finance director.' She prayed that Helen wouldn't stay. She didn't think she could bear to see them together.

'Really?' Helen's green eyes were icy. 'Judging by the touching farewell I just witnessed, I expected he'd gone away for at least a week!'

'I'm sorry?'

'Don't give me that innocent look! I saw you through that glass panel in the door. I saw Luke kissing you and that silly besotted look on your face,' Helen sneered. Seeing the flush stain Kate's cheeks, she pursued her advantage. 'And I thought you were supposed to be the ultimate professional secretary! I could have told Luke that you'd turn out like all the others!'

Kate went still. 'What others?'

'*What others*?' Helen mimicked spitefully. 'Did you really think you were special? Why do you think he's had so many secretaries?'

'He's a difficult man.' Kate had herself well under control now. 'They couldn't cope with him.'

'Is that what he told you? And you believed it?' Helen strolled insolently over to the window and lit a cigarette with sinuous grace. 'You little fool!' she jeered, blowing out a cloud of smoke. 'All his secretaries start off being efficient little madams like you, and they all fall for him in the end. It's just a question of time before they start throwing themselves at him; you must have lasted longer than most.'

She turned round and inspected Kate with contempt. 'Luke, as you have no doubt discovered, is not a man to resist a woman offered to him on a plate, but after a while he gets bored and it all gets rather embarrassing. When it comes down to it he only loves this wretched firm, and the last thing he wants is some secretary getting involved and emotional. They always leave in tears, and he comes back to me. We understand each other.'

'Good for you,' Kate said evenly, but her eyes flashed with dislike as she turned deliberately away. Helen's words had hit her like sharp little stones, but she would have died rather than admit how much they hurt.

As she turned her back Helen drew a sudden breath. 'Catherine Haddington-Finch,' she said slowly. 'That's who you are! I knew I'd seen you somewhere before!'

Kate froze. 'I don't know what you're talking about.'

'Oh, yes, you do!' Helen stubbed out her cigarette and came back from the window. 'I thought you looked familiar, but as soon as I saw that look of disgust I knew where I'd seen you. You were Anne's ugly little friend at Chittingdene. I always thought it was a joke that you—you!— dared to disapprove of me. You were always so quiet, but you had a special little contemptuous look you kept for me.'

She walked round to face Kate. 'Yes, it's obvious now. You've filled out, of course, but get rid of that rather smart hairstyle and put those terrible bottle-bottom glasses back on and you'd look just the same!' Her smile was cold, malicious, as she circled Kate speculatively. 'Well, well. Catherine Haddington-Finch! Who would have thought it? Does Luke know?'

'No,' said Kate quietly. It was useless to deny it all now.

'I always thought you had rather a crush on him,' Helen went on. 'Anne told me you actually went down to tell him I wasn't coming that day. Rather touching.'

Her mockery caught Kate on the raw. 'You didn't really want him then, did you?' she said angrily. 'You were just playing with him. Anne told me what you used to say about Luke behind his back. Why do you want him so much now?'

Helen shrugged, unperturbed. 'He was a little rough in those days, and I had a better offer in mind. But now, well, he's a very attractive man.'

'And a very rich one?'

'You always did have a sharp tongue for someone so plain, Catherine,' Helen said with dislike.

'At least it was an honest one,' Kate retorted. 'I never pretended to be in love with Luke and then sneered at him when he wasn't there.'

Helen gave a harsh laugh. 'Love? Luke isn't interested in love! He doesn't give a damn what people think about him.'

'Not now he doesn't, but that's because thoughtless, cruel girls like you taught him that love was worthless. No wonder he's cynical!' Kate's eyes were blazing. 'Didn't it ever occur to you that he might be hurt by the way you treated him? But no, you had a better offer, and you couldn't even be bothered to say goodbye!'

'Luke didn't care,' Helen said lightly. 'If he did, why would he keep coming back to me?'

'At least he knows what he's dealing with,' Kate said with a contempt that made Helen's green eyes flash.

'Which is more than he does with you, Little Miss Virtue! It's all very well for you to preach about honesty, but how honest is it to keep your identity a secret?'

'It's not a secret. Luke didn't recognise me, and I didn't see any point in reminding him. I'm sure he wouldn't remember me anyway.'

'No, probably not,' Helen said dismissively. 'You weren't exactly the memorable type.'

'You remembered me,' Kate pointed out. 'And I've changed. I'm not the plain, awkward little girl I was. I'd like Luke to remember me as I am now, not as I was. I think he will—especially after last night,' she added deliberately.

Helen's eyes narrowed. 'If you think one night gives you any hold over Luke, you've got another think coming! I give you a week before Luke asks you to leave.'

'I wouldn't give you that long if Luke comes back now,' Kate said with a coolness that surprised her. 'He won't want a scene in the office, and, in view of last night, I think he's likely to take my side in any argument.' She picked up the pile of letters from her desk and began to slit them open. 'I suggest you leave now—and don't come back until there's another secretary sitting here!'

'That won't be long!' Helen said viciously and stormed out of the office, letting the door bang noisily behind her.

Left unexpectedly holding the field, Kate realised that she was shaking. She sat down abruptly in her chair and dropped her head in her hands.

Was she just the latest in a line of over-emotional secretaries? Was that all she was to Luke? Kate didn't want to believe Helen, but the story wasn't that unlikely, after all. Luke himself had mentioned her tearful predecessors: was it so incredible that they had fallen in love with him? *She* had; why shouldn't they?

Kate pulled her fingers through her hair. It was soft and gleaming still, just as it had been when Luke had tangled his fingers in it and tilted her head back for his kiss. The memory of the night they had shared tore at her. It was impossible to believe it hadn't meant anything to Luke. She couldn't mistake the look in his eyes or the tenderness of his touch.

No, she wouldn't believe Helen, but she would have to tell Luke about Chittingdene now. If only she had told him last night! She dreaded the confession in the cold light of day. He would want to know why she hadn't told him before, and it would be hard to explain without sounding deceitful or, worse, calculating.

And then the door opened and Luke came in. One look at his face told Kate that her confession would be unnecessary.

'I met Helen on her way out,' he said heavily. His expression was tight and closed. 'She said you were Catherine Haddington-Finch from Chittingdene. Is it true?'

Kate lifted her head and met his eyes squarely. 'What do you think?'

'Catherine?' he said, as if wanting to disbelieve. He searched her face, and then sighed as he read the truth in her eyes. 'Catherine.'

'Kate,' she corrected him quietly.

'Why didn't you tell me?' He turned away, unable to hide the bitterness in his face.

'There never seemed to be an opportunity,' she began, but he interrupted her.

'An opportunity! You never had any trouble talking to me about anything else!'

'This was different. I didn't think you'd remember me anyway. Why should you?'

'I remember you all right. You were the girl who came down to the wood to tell me about Helen.'

Kate nodded miserably. 'But you didn't recognise me. I didn't see any point in bringing up the past. You made it pretty clear you'd put it behind you, and I thought it would just be embarrassing for both of us.'

'I suppose you thought I might be embarrassed at having the daughter of the manor at my beck and call? Was that it?'

'No!' Kate's heart sank at the harsh note in his voice. 'I was remembering that day in the woods. The last time I saw you you kissed me. It seemed an awkward memory for a boss and a secretary to share, that's all.'

'And all those times I wondered if I'd met you before? Did you have a good snigger then? That Frenchwoman I told you about in the restaurant; she was your mother, wasn't she? That must have had you in stitches!'

'No! Luke, you know I've never laughed at you.'

'The trouble is, I *don't* know about you any more.' He turned away angrily. 'I really thought you were different. When I looked into those clear eyes of yours I thought I saw only honesty. You've made a fool out of me, haven't you? You're just as deceitful as all the others!'

Kate lifted her chin. 'I've never lied to you.'

'It doesn't seem that way to me. Keeping something like that secret is just as dishonest.'

'It never seemed to bother you about Helen!' Kate cried. 'What about all the things she didn't tell you?'

'Helen's different. I never expected anything from her, but you...you were special, Kate. At least, I thought you were.' He laughed mirthlessly.

Kate was angry now. 'What about all those other secretaries you seduced? I suppose they were all special too? It must save you so much effort, using the same line every time!'

'What other secretaries?' Luke demanded, swinging round.

'Helen told me. Apparently I'm just the latest in a long line of secretaries to fall for your line about being the best ever!'

'And you believe what Helen says?'

'You appear to!'

They were both too angry to hear the door open. One of the junior secretaries stood in the doorway, clutching some files, startled and embarrassed by the scene that met her eyes.

'Get out!' Luke snarled, and she turned and fled.

'I see you're back to being your usual charming self!' snapped Kate.

'When are you going to revert to being Catherine Haddington-Finch? I'm surprised I didn't remember as soon as you started bossing me around! You're just like your father, that pompous old fool, playing squire up at the manor.'

'My father was not pompous!' Kate hissed. 'He was kind and generous, which is more than you are! You've just got some stupid chip on your shoulder. What does it matter if I was called Catherine and lived in a big house? We've both grown up since then. Surely it's who we are now that matters?'

Luke was standing by the window, glaring down at the street, a tic jumping in his jaw. 'That's just it. I thought I knew who you were, but now I find that you're someone completely different.' He glanced over his shoulder at Kate, who was rigid beside her desk, her tawny eyes ablaze. 'I was going to ask the girl called Kate to marry me tonight. Quite a joke, isn't it?' His face was closed and bitter. 'But I don't feel like marrying Catherine. She might have other secrets she doesn't want me to know.'

Kate looked at the back of his head in despair. 'I'm not Catherine, I'm Kate. If you can dismiss the Kate you've known after the last few weeks that easily I don't want to marry you! Can you dismiss last night too? Did it seem to you that we had any secrets that mattered then?' Luke stiffened but didn't turn round. 'There are lots of things I don't know about you,' she went on. 'For all I know, you have been seducing secretaries for the last ten years, but if you'd asked me to set that against what I learnt of you last night I'd have said it didn't matter.'

Angry tears were very close, and she scrabbled frantically for her bag. 'Still, I'm sure you'll find another *special* secretary soon to console you. Make sure you check her birth certificate before you employ her!' Determined not to cry in front of him, she snatched up her coat as Luke spun round.

'Where do you think you're going?'

'I'm leaving.' Kate stormed over to the door. 'You can deal with your own rotten contract and learn to speak French yourself!'

Slamming the door behind her, she jabbed at the lift button. It *would* be on the ground floor! 'Come on, come on!' she prayed as it inched its way upwards with an infuriating lack of haste.

'Kate!' Luke called from the office doorway.

'It's Kate now, is it? It was Catherine a minute ago!' Kate shouted, oblivious of the fact that their voices were echoing down the corridor and would be heard in all the offices.

'You needn't think you can just storm off like this,' Luke yelled back. 'You're under contract.'

'You know what you can do with your precious contract!' Kate hit the lift button with her fist, glancing over her shoulder in panic as she saw Luke advancing towards her. If he touched her she was lost. 'Come *on!*'

At last there was a ping, and the lift doors slid open laboriously. Kate practically fell inside and jammed the 'close doors' button, missing the fact that Luke veered off and ran for the stairs.

As the doors closed behind her Kate's knees began to shake, and she leant back against the mirrored wall, pressing her hand against her face to hold back the sobs that threatened to tear her apart.

It was a slow lift at the best of times, stopping at every floor. Somebody must have pressed all the buttons as a practical joke. Kate was glad that no one wanted to share the lift, and she tried desperately to pull herself together as the doors opened at the ground floor.

To her horror, Luke stood there in front of a cluster of people waiting for the lift. He was out of breath and panting, barring her escape.

Kate tried to push past him, but he caught her and dragged her back into the lift, pushing her against the mirror and kissing her fiercely. She put her hands up to resist and jammed them against his chest, but he was too strong for her. He held her head between his hands, ignoring her struggles, and kissed her, deep, desperate kisses that crumbled her resistance and woke a fire of response where anger and bitter unhappiness melted into the absolute certainty of love.

He could feel the change in her, for his hands left her face, sliding down her back to wrap her closely to him. Kate's arms were about his neck as she kissed him back. Without a word's being said, all was explained and understood and forgiven.

'Let's go back upstairs,' Luke said, raising his head at last. He turned round to press the button for the fourth floor and to face an interested audience in the reception area.

'You'll have to wait,' he said, taking Kate back into his arms. 'This one's full.'

Back on the fourth floor, there were little knots of people in the office doorways, all clearly discussing the scene that had taken place, for they fell silent abruptly as Luke and Kate reappeared.

'Why aren't you all working?' Luke demanded. 'I don't pay you to stand around gossiping all day!'

Everyone moved hastily, but Kate could just imagine the raised eyebrows as he took her hand and dragged her down to their office so fast that she had to trot to keep up.

Pushing her into his inner office, he shut the door firmly behind him and looked at her.

'Now, what do you mean by storming off like that?'

'What do you mean by dragging me back like that?' Kate retorted, thoroughly ruffled and unsure of whether she felt deliriously happy or cross.

Luke took her hands and held them tightly as he looked into her eyes. 'I mean that I'm sorry,' he said simply. 'I mean that I love you. I mean that I'm not letting you go again. Is that clear enough?'

Kate couldn't speak. She could only nod, her eyes golden and starry with relief.

'I really am sorry, Kate,' Luke went on seriously. 'When I saw you get into that lift I suddenly realised what a fool I'd been and that if I let you go like that it would be the worst thing I'd ever done. I've never run so fast as I did down those stairs; I was terrified you'd leave before I caught you, so I called the lift at every floor in the hope of slowing you down. I only just made it in time.'

He paused. 'I don't know why I blew my top like that. After last night I was sure of what I'd suspected for a long time—that you were the only woman for me. It was just such a shock to suddenly find that you were someone completely different.'

'I'm sorry too,' Kate said. 'I should have told you, but I didn't want to spoil things. I wanted you to think of me as the woman I am now, not the girl I was then. I didn't think you'd want to remember kissing that plain, scrawny girl.'

'I didn't, but not for the reason you think,' Luke said slowly. 'I wished I hadn't taken my anger with Helen out on you. Afterwards it was hard to forget the look in your eyes when I let you go. In later years, whenever I did something I wasn't very proud of I'd remember that look.'

Kate smiled. 'I'm glad you remembered. That was my first kiss, Luke. Nobody ever kissed me like that. I think I've been in love with you ever since.'

'Do you love me now, even after the way I've shouted at you and bullied you?'

'More than ever,' she said, and he caught her to him for a kiss that went on and on in the giddy exhilaration of knowing that everything was going to be all right.

'Luke?' Kate said later. She was sitting on his lap on one of the squashy leather chairs she had avoided during her interview, and her fingers were curling round his. 'Why did you take up with Helen again? She was so cruel to you before.'

Luke stroked her face with such tenderness that her heart ached. 'Why? I think I had some vague thought of getting my own back on her. She's not nearly as cool as she likes to make out, and she wants marriage just as much as anyone else. I have to admit I took some amusement from beating her at her own game, stringing her along and then suddenly taking up with someone else. Besides, you were right, I have had a bit of a chip on my shoulder for a long time, and Helen is . . . well, she's very beautiful. She was good for my image.'

'I told her not to come back while I was still your secretary,' Kate confessed.

'I know. She told me. She was furious with you when she met me in the corridor and dropped the bombshell about who you were. I think she must have realised how much you meant to me, because she told me what she said to you about my previous secretaries—all nonsense, of course. There's only one secretary who's ever made me realise that all the attempts I'd made to stay cynical and detached were just a pretence.'

'What happened to her?' Kate asked innocently.

'Oh, I sacked her.'

'You *what*?' Kate sat up, indignant, but Luke pulled her back against him. 'I decided she was just too distracting at the office. In any case, her talents could be put to better use elsewhere.'

She eyed him speculatively. 'Where?'

'In my home and in my heart,' Luke said, and tightened his arms about her. 'Marry me, Kate,' he demanded, suddenly urgent, and then, with a smile that sent shivers of anticipation down her spine, '*please*?'

Kate rested her face against his neck and sighed with happiness. 'Since you ask so nicely...yes.'

'Yes what?' said Luke, pretending to be shocked.

'Yes, please.'

Let

HARLEQUIN ROMANCE®

take you

BACK TO THE RANCH

Come to the Lucky Horseshoe Ranch, near Pepper, Texas!

Meet Cody Bailman—cattle rancher, single father and Texan—and Sherry Waterman, a nurse-midwife who's new to town.

Read LONE STAR LOVIN' by Debbie Macomber, July's Back to the Ranch title!

Available wherever Harlequin Books are sold.

RANCH2

**Relive the romance...
Harlequin and Silhouette
are proud to present**

by Request

A program of collections of three complete novels by the most requested authors with the most requested themes. Be sure to look for one volume each month with three complete novels by top name authors.

In June: **NINE MONTHS** Penny Jordan
Stella Cameron
Janice Kaiser

Three women pregnant and alone. But a lot can happen in nine months!

In July: **DADDY'S HOME** Kristin James
Naomi Horton
Mary Lynn Baxter

Daddy's Home... and his presence is long overdue!

In August: **FORGOTTEN PAST** Barbara Kaye
Pamela Browning
Nancy Martin

Do you dare to create a future if you've forgotten the past?

Available at your favorite retail outlet.

Harlequin is proud to present our best authors and their best books. Always the best for your reading pleasure!

Throughout 1993, Harlequin will bring you exciting books by some of the top names in contemporary romance!

In July look for *The Ties That Bind* by

Shannon wanted him seven days a week....

Dark, compelling, mysterious Garth Sheridan was no mere boy next door—even if he did rent the cottage beside Shannon Raine's.

She was intrigued by the hard-nosed exec, but for Shannon it was all or nothing. Either break the undeniable bonds between them... or tear down the barriers surrounding Garth and discover the truth.

Don't miss **THE TIES THAT BIND** ... wherever Harlequin books are sold.

Fifty red-blooded, white-hot, true-blue hunks from every
State in the Union!

Beginning in May, look for MEN MADE IN AMERICA!
Written by some of our most popular authors, these
stories feature fifty of the strongest, sexiest men, each
from a different state in the union!

Two titles available every other month at your favorite
retail outlet.

In July, look for:

CALL IT DESTINY by Jayne Ann Krentz (Arizona)
ANOTHER KIND OF LOVE by Mary Lynn Baxter
(Arkansas)

In September, look for:

DECEPTIONS by Annette Broadrick (California)
STORMWALKER by Dallas Schulze (Colorado)

You won't be able to resist MEN MADE IN AMERICA!

THREE UNFORGETTABLE HEROINES
THREE AWARD-WINNING AUTHORS

Untamed

MAVERICK HEARTS

A unique collection of historical short stories that capture the spirit of America's last frontier.

HEATHER GRAHAM POZZESSERE—over 10 million copies of her books in print worldwide
Lonesome Rider—The story of an Eastern widow and the renegade half-breed who becomes her protector.

PATRICIA POTTER—an author whose books are consistently Waldenbooks bestsellers
Against the Wind—Two people, battered by heartache, prove that love can heal all.

JOAN JOHNSTON—award-winning Western historical author with 17 books to her credit
One Simple Wish—A woman with a past discovers that dreams really do come true.

Join us for an exciting journey West with
UNTAMED
Available in July, wherever Harlequin books are sold.